Sweet Dreams

GOLDEN GIRL

Jane Ballard

BANTAM BOOKS

NEW YORK · TORONTO · LONDON · SYDNEY · AUCKLAND

GOLDEN GIRL

A BANTAM BOOK 0 553 28348 0

First publication in Great Britain

PRINTING HISTORY
Bantam edition published 1991

Bantam Books are published by Transworld Publishers Ltd.,
61–63 Uxbridge Road, Ealing, London W5 5SA,
in Australia by Transworld Publishers (Australia) Pty. Ltd.,
15–23 Helles Avenue, Moorebank, NSW 2170, and in New
Zealand by Transworld Publishers (N.Z.) Ltd., Cnr. Moselle
and Waipareira Avenues, Henderson, Auckland.

Made and printed in Great Britain by
BPCC Hazell Books
Aylesbury, Bucks, England
Member of BPCC Ltd.

To my editor, Ruth Koeppel

Chapter One

I can't believe I'm going through with this. I must be nuts.

I wiped my damp palms on my new wool skirt and took a deep, calming breath. When I'd arrived at KIRQ-TV twenty minutes earlier, the receptionist had handed me a sheet describing the competition rules and told me to have a seat in the waiting room. I found myself reading the first sentence over and over again, but I just couldn't concentrate on the words.

I kept wondering if my ash blond, shoulder-length hair looked okay, and whether my new peach eye shadow complemented my hazel eyes. I hoped my mascara wasn't smudged under my eyes—sometimes it does that and I look like a football player who's protecting his eyes from sun glare.

I could see a distorted, golden version of

myself in the shiny brass lamp on the table next to me. I didn't see any smudges in my reflection, but I rubbed a finger quickly under both eyes just in case.

Across the waiting room from me sat Lana Boyson. I felt my spirits sink as I watched her chatting with two of her friends. She had huge, blue eyes and long, thick, golden blond hair that tumbled down her back in beautiful waves. She was a cheerleader, of course, and a senior in my brother's class at Lincoln High School. I concentrated on *not* looking at them so I wouldn't get too psyched out by the competition.

What in the world was I doing there? I hadn't competed for anything since the sixth-grade spelling bee! And here I was, auditioning for the most glamorous job in town—the "Golden Girl" for Trent's Department Store. Every year a local high school girl was chosen to be the spokesperson for the store in its television commercials and print ads, and every year at least two hundred girls tried out for the job.

"I just know they'll prefer a blond!" Lana gushed, running her fingers through her hair. She looked as if she were doing a commercial for hair conditioner or shampoo or something, the way she tipped her head to one side and let her hair cascade over one shoulder. "Last year, they had to pick a dark-haired girl, Jennie Reeves, because she was the prettiest girl who applied. But the title 'Golden Girl' implies that a blond would be most suitable, don't you think?"

"They *usually* chose a blond," one of her friends said. "Last year was unusual. But the thing is that they want talent, too. The Golden Girl has to do a commercial twice a month for a year, so you've got to know how to act in front of a camera."

Lana smiled knowingly. "I've been practicing in the bathroom mirror for *years*—I've always known I'd be a star!"

I rolled my eyes and thought, *Get me out of here!*

"You're Joe Montgomery's sister, aren't you?" The voice was Lana's and obviously directed at me.

"Yes," I said, looking up and meeting those cool blue eyes.

"I'm surprised to see you here. Aren't you on the newspaper staff or something like that?" The way she'd said newspaper staff made it sound like a leper colony. No one in Lana's clique would be caught dead on the newspaper staff—cheerleading and pompons were more their style.

I felt my body stiffen. "I'm poetry editor for the literary magazine."

Lana smirked and raised her eyebrows. "Well, I don't think the Golden Girl job will call for reciting much poetry."

Lana's friends laughed, obviously appreciating her obnoxious joke.

From where I was sitting, I could see the parking lot through the large glass doors of the television station. *Would anyone notice if I ran out screaming into the street? I wondered. Why did I let Joe talk me into this?*

Actually, my brother had *dared* me to audition. And as ridiculous as it sounds, I haven't been able to pass up a dare from Joe since we were little kids.

But as I sat there in the waiting room, I realized what a mistake it had been to agree to this audition. To be perfectly honest, I look okay, but there was no way that my face and body could compete with Lana Boyson's and come out ahead. I was certain that they'd choose someone from Joe's class who already looked good enough to be a cover girl.

"They'll pick someone who is beautiful, talented, poised, and very sure of herself," Lana said, looking at me pointedly. "Someone who's had experience performing." The last time I made a speech in front of an audience was last year in ninth grade. Ms. Simms had had my language arts class memorize a soliloquy of our choice from one of Shakespeare's plays. I chose Ophelia's mad scene from *Hamlet*. It was supposed to be dramatic, Ophelia going mad and all, but I had my classmates rolling in the aisles with hysterical laughter. I was

4

so nervous that the moment I reached the front of the classroom, I'd come down with a case of the hiccups.

An assistant entered the room and handed out audition scripts to all of us. I looked down at the paper in my hand and forced myself to concentrate on the words.

Do we have a sale for you! Twenty percent off all items in junior and petite sizes at Trent's Department Store. Come in and see all the styles and colors we have for our winter fashions! But you'd better hurry! Prices like these won't last long!

It didn't seem like reading this commercial would be anywhere near as hard as reading Shakespeare, but I was even more nervous. With all those exclamation marks, I figured they were expecting a very animated reading. I took out a pencil and underlined the words I thought I should emphasize and made little arrows pointing up or down where I intended to raise or lower my pitch.

Now if I could just get through it without getting a case of the hiccups. I was trembling the way I had last year in Ms. Simms's class. *Déjà vu.*

A few minutes later there was a clatter of footsteps in the hall, and all the girls in the waiting room froze. A tall blond woman appeared, then glanced down at the clipboard that she held in her hand.

"Claire Montgomery?"

"Yes?" The word slipped out, sounding more like a gasp than an answer.

"You're next." She smiled, displaying small, perfectly formed teeth. Her smile would have been perfect if her teeth weren't covered with tobacco stains. That seemed to be her only flaw, since she looked and moved like a model.

"Please follow me," she said. "Bring your coat and leave the copy here; you won't need it."

I glanced around. "The copy of what?"

Lana and her friends collapsed in a fit of giggles.

"The copy," she said. "The script you just read for the commercial is called 'copy.' "

"Oh." I could feel my face heating up as the three girls continued to smile smugly. They probably thought that my mistake would count against me in the audition.

"Good luck," Lana said, still smiling. "I hope you do well."

Right, I thought, *and crocodiles make great pets.* . . .

"Thanks," I said, following the woman with the blond hair down the hall.

It was too late to escape now. I'd missed my chance, and now I would have to go through with the audition. The woman led me to a set of double doors.

"You can go right on in," she said, giving me an encouraging smile.

I forced myself to pull the door open and walked into the studio. It felt cooler in there and was quite dark, except for some studio lights in one far corner of the large room. The lights focused on a roll of blue material that hung down like a movie screen that was too long and dragged on the floor. One camera was directed at the screen.

It was kind of creepy stepping into the dark room. My eyes needed time to adjust to the dark after being in the brightly lit waiting room. I wasn't even sure if I was alone or not.

Suddenly I heard a rustling noise, and I jumped at least two inches off the floor. I glanced to my right in the direction of the sound and thought I saw the figure of a man sitting in a chair. The studio lighting was behind him, so all I could see was his silhouette. If this had been an old Alfred Hitchcock movie, he'd have risen from his seat in the dark and come after me with a butcher knife.

I didn't see any knives, but I was nervous just the same.

Then he spoke. "Tell me what time it is, and I'll tell you who you are."

It was a young man's voice, and I was relieved that he didn't sound much like the killer type.

"Huh?"

"I have a schedule here that identifies each girl by the time of her appointment. What time is it?" he asked. "My watch is in the shop."

"Um, well, my appointment was for four o'clock. . . ."

He consulted a loose-leaf notebook on his lap.

"Well, that means you're Claire Montgomery."

"Yes."

"Come closer so I can see you."

I walked to within a few feet of his chair, then took a look at him. My eyes were adjusted by now to the dimly lit studio, but I blinked several times to make sure I was seeing right.

He was about seventeen, with dark hair, blue eyes, and the arms and chest of a weight lifter. In short, dreamboat material. Even after I'd blinked several times, he was still there and still just as gorgeous.

"How old are you, Claire?" His tone was friendly, almost intimate. It's not something I experience every day with the boys my age, and my stomach did a little flip.

"Fifteen."

They usually pick juniors or seniors, I remembered too late. *Maybe I should have lied about my age. Oh, who cares? I'm not going to be picked anyway!*

"Um-hmm," he said, making a notation. "Have you had any performing experience?"

"I played Ophelia once." *Oh, boy, that's really pushing it!*

"Impressive," he said, smiling at me. "You seem a little nervous, Claire. This will be painless, I promise."

"Who, me? Nervous?" I squeaked, amazed that he'd bought my story. A giggle slipped out accidentally. "I'm not nat all nervous."

Not nat all nervous? Come on! I could feel my cheeks turning red.

He laughed, but I thought how nice it sounded. He wasn't putting me down; he was just trying to help me feel less nervous. "Let me tell you a little about what's going on here."

"Okay," I said.

"My father is the executive producer of the Trent's Department Store commercials. He asked me to choose the top five applicants—a rough job."

"Really?" I said.

He grinned. "Sure. Interviewing hundreds of beautiful girls. It's a tough job, but somebody's got to do it."

It was my turn to laugh now. "I see."

He got up from his chair and approached me. He smiled and looked deep into my eyes and extended his hand. "I'm Ben Riley."

If this had been a Broadway musical, the

studio set would've faded away at that moment, swirls of fog would have surrounded me, and I'd have started singing about love at first sight.

Ben Riley. Wow.

"It's nice to meet you," I said, shaking his hand. "I'm Claire—" I stopped. "Oh, right, you already know my name." I felt like the color of my face turned from red to purple at that point.

Ben placed a hand on my shoulder. "Hey, you'll be fine. Are you ready?"

"Sure, of course. No problem."

Ben gestured to a lighted window above us.

"Who's that?" I blurted out when I looked in the direction he'd indicated.

"The engineer," he said. "He's waiting for us."

Ben pointed to the blue screen in the lighted area. "Go stand over there. There's a mark on the floor in front of the screen. That's your spot."

"Okay." I walked over to the masking-tape X on the floor and faced the camera.

"Did you get a chance to study the copy?" Ben asked.

"Yes," I said. "I did that while I was in the waiting room." I mentally thanked the blond woman for letting me know what "copy" was.

"Good. Look into the lense of the camera, and you'll see the TelePrompTer," Ben said.

I looked into the camera. Just over the lense were the first few lines of the commercial projected on a square screen.

"Can you see the copy?" Ben asked.

"Hey, yeah. That's really neat." *Neat? You sure aren't going to get this job if you sound like a little kid!* I chided myself.

"Go ahead and read it through," Ben said. He slipped on a headset and watched me through the camera.

"Okay," I said. I watched the camera lense and read the lines to myself again.

"Claire," Ben said after a moment.

"Yes?"

"Read it *out loud*."

"Oh. Right." *He must think I'm a moron!*

So I read it aloud, and as I got to the last words that I could see on the TelePrompTer, the lines crawled slowly up the screen, revealing more of the commercial copy. I continued reading it to the last sentence.

"Okay, but you read it in a flat voice," Ben said with a slow smile. "Now read it as if you're giving a performance."

"At least I didn't get the hiccups," I mumbled.

"What?"

"Nothing. I'll try it again."

"Whenever you're ready."

This time when I read, I remembered what I'd worked on in the waiting room. I emphasized the important words and tried to vary

11

the pitch of my voice to make the reading more interesting. It was funny, but when I concentrated on the words, I felt less nervous.

"Pretty good," Ben said, stroking his chin thoughtfully as he studied my face. "You knew instinctively what words to emphasize, and you kept your eyes still while you read the TelePrompTer. A lot of people don't think about that. Good job." He paused, then signaled the engineer in the lighted window.

"Let's do a take this time. I need much more enthusiasm. Much more. Persuade me to come with you to the sale." He smiled. "Tempt me."

"Okay," I said, "you asked for it!"

I read it again, and this time I pretended that I was a beautiful, sexy woman from a soap opera wearing a formal evening gown. Okay, so it was a ridiculous idea, but it made the reading fun.

I really got into it. In fact, I got into it so much that I kind of got carried away and did something that I still can't believe. When I read the last two lines—"But you'd better hurry! Prices like these won't last long!"—I went right ahead and added a line of my own, still in my soap opera character: "*I'll* be there, and I can't *wait* to see you!"

I couldn't believe I'd actually done it. At least no one could ever say that I don't have guts!

Ben came around in front of the camera with a grin on his face.

"You persuaded me," he said, gazing at me in astonishment. "I'd follow you anywhere, even though I've heard those lines before!"

Well, *his* lines took the breath right out of me, let me tell you. No boy had ever talked to me that way before.

Ben squeezed my arm. "We're through. That was terrific. My dad and Mr. Trent will be making the final decision tomorrow and I'll call you either way."

"Thanks, Ben," I managed to say as I picked up my coat and walked out through the double doors in a daze, through the waiting room, and into the late afternoon sunshine.

I'd follow you anywhere.

That one sentence and the memory of his intense blue eyes overwhelmed me, blocking out everything else, as I made my way home.

I walked the mile home in my heels. Actually, I *limped* home in the thirty-five degree weather, but I didn't even care. All I could think of was Ben Riley and how he would follow me anywhere.

I staggered up the wooden porch steps, pushed open the front door, and collapsed in a happy heap on the carpeted stairs near the front closet.

Chapter Two

My feet were absolutely killing me. I took off my shoes and threw them into the living room, unable to believe that some people wore high-heeled shoes to work every day.

The house was quiet. The sun was sinking lower and lower in the sky, and the light that slanted in through the front windows created bright squares on the hardwood floor. I leaned against the heavy wooden bannister, exhausted from my trek home. Then I bent over to rub my toes and groaned.

"Hi, Care."

I didn't need to turn around to know who it was. Joe was coming in from the kitchen, his favorite room in the house. He's called me Care ever since he was two years old. Mom tells me that when she brought me home from the hospital, she called to him to come and see his little sister, Claire. He ran down the porch steps to the car and peered into my face and said exactly what he said just now: "Hi, Care." I guess the name just stuck.

I didn't bother to answer his greeting. If it hadn't been for his stupid dare, I wouldn't have aching feet right now. Okay, I wouldn't have met Ben Riley either, I know, but for now I purposely overlooked that small detail. I was prepared to milk this for all it was worth.

I moaned louder and twisted my face into an exaggerated grimace.

"What's wrong with you?" Joe asked.

"Ooh, my feeeet!" I gasped.

"What's the matter with 'em?" he asked. He loped over and stood next to me, polishing off a can of soda.

Joe is tall and my friends tell me he's really a hunk, but I don't know what they're talking about. He's totally aggravating at least eighty percent of the time. During the other twenty percent, he's asleep or eating. He's a blue-eyed blond and not what you'd call a great student, but he's the star of the high school swim team. Three of my friends actually went to a swim meet for the sole purpose of getting a look at Joe. I couldn't believe it! There's just no accounting for taste, I guess.

I glared up at him. "What do you *think* is the matter with them?"

It was only then that he noticed what I was

wearing. "You look good for a change, Care. What happened?" He leaned over and tugged at a strand of my hair.

I let out an exasperated cry. "You mean, you don't *remember*? You don't remember the dare?"

Joe looked like he was trying to think. "Which one?"

I stared up at him as he loomed over me but couldn't tell if he really couldn't remember or if he was putting me on.

"You dared me to audition for the Trent's Golden Girl job!" I cried. "I can't believe this! I didn't even *want* to do it! I exposed myself to the ridicule of your snotty classmates, took the risk of making an absolute *fool* out of myself, completely *wasted* a whole afternoon, and got so incredibly *nervous*, all for—" I stopped ranting for a moment, and lowered my voice for dramatic effect. "I put myself through all that because of your stupid dare and you don't even remember it!"

Joe smiled a little. "Oh, yeah," he said, and plopped down on the step next to me. "*That* dare. How'd it go?"

I smiled smugly. "I was terrific."

"Oh, yeah?"

"Yeah. I was soooo good, Joe," I said. "I think I really impressed the producer."

"Oh, yeah?" Joe said again. "Who's that?"

"Well, actually, he's the son of the executive

16

producer. His name is Ben Riley. He's a few years older than I am. He ran the audition."

"Ben Riley?" Joe took a swig of soda. "Yeah, I know who he is."

I immediately became very alert. "You *do*? You know Ben Riley? Dark hair, blue eyes, *incredible* body? That Ben Riley?"

Joe leaned back lazily against the wall and grinned. "Well, dark hair and blue eyes, anyway." He took another drink.

I grabbed the can out of his hand. "What's he like? Tell me about him! Is he in any of your classes?"

Joe looked angry. "Hey, give that back!" I passed the can of soda back to him and he stared at me a minute. "Why are you asking me all these questions?"

I sat back again. "No reason," I said. "Just curious, that's all."

A slow smile crept across Joe's face. He shrugged. "He's just a guy. No big deal."

"Maybe not to you," I said under my breath.

He continued to grin at me for a moment. Then he wiped his mouth on the back of his hand and looked at me thoughtfully.

"You really tried out 'cause of my dare?"

"Yeah," I said, proud of myself. "And I was a big hit, as if I'd been acting in TV commercials all my life."

He scratched the side of his face. He hadn't shaved for a couple of days, and I think his whiskers were beginning to itch. "So are you going to be the next Golden Girl?"

I laughed. "Are you kidding? Of course not."

Joe looked puzzled. "I thought you said you were terrific."

"I *was*—I mean I was good for *me*. But I can't compete with Lana Boyson."

"Did Lana try out?"

I nodded.

Joe smiled. "So what did Ben Riley say?"

"What do you mean?" I asked.

"About your audition," Joe said. "What did he say?"

"He said I was terrific," I said. "But he probably says that to every girl who tries out."

Joe laughed. "Yeah, you're right, he probably does."

I was crushed. "Really? You mean you think he wasn't sincere? You think he really says that to everyone?"

"Oh, he wouldn't say that to just anyone," Joe said, punching me playfully in the arm. "Only the cute girls." He stopped and looked at me with an exaggerated frown. "So I wonder why he said that to *you*."

I groaned and collapsed back onto the stairs. "You're incorrigible," I said.

"Thanks, I work at it," he said, grinning.

Joe stretched his right arm up and back behind his head, with his elbow bent. I recognized it as one of the warm-up exercises he does before swimming practice.

"Are you leaving?" I asked.

"Yeah. I've got practice." He circled his arm around like a pinwheel at his side. "Gotta go."

"Okay," I said. "But promise me you'll tell me everything you know about Ben Riley."

"I can't wait," he said, rolling his eyes. "See you later, Care." He shrugged on his coat and disappeared out the front door.

After he drove away, I got up from the steps. I live in a small Tudor-style house. The rooms are tiny but neat—no thanks to my brother— with hardwood floors and old-fashioned stuffed couches and chairs. The rest of the furniture is antique. Mom is the sort of person who loves to go to garage sales, pick up old furniture and refinish it.

Mom was busy in the kitchen chopping vegetables for dinner when I walked in. She was wearing jeans and a sweatshirt, and she was barefoot, revealing her bright red toenails.

"Dinner will be ready in an hour," she chirped. "Lentil nut loaf."

I sighed. *Why couldn't I have a mom who fixed normal suppers like fried chicken or Tater Tot casserole?*

"Oh, I nearly forgot!" she said, turning to me from the kitchen counter. "How was the audition?"

I filled her in, leaving out the romantic parts in case nothing ever happened between

Ben and me. I told her that even though I had done an incredibly good job at the audition, I didn't expect to be chosen because of the stiff competition.

Joe may have very little confidence in me, but Mom is entirely different. She thinks I could pick up an Academy Award, accept the Nobel Peace Prize, and be crowned Miss America all on the same day if I only had the time.

"Oh, honey, you're a beautiful girl," she said. "You have just as good a chance as that Lorna person."

"Lana Boyson, Mom," I corrected.

"You're beautiful, you're talented, you're *very* smart—"

"Thanks, Mom," I said. "I appreciate your support. But no offense, you don't know what you're talking about. You're my mother." She looked surprised, so I decided to explain. "Mom, Lana is—well, she's like . . . like Helen of Troy, the kind of girl that men start wars over."

She smiled lovingly at me, "So are you."

I rolled my eyes. "Thanks, Mom, but you're totally biased. See you at dinner."

She cheerfully blew me a kiss and I headed up to my room. I wanted to replay the audition over and over in my mind and think about Ben Riley.

I lay on my bed and fantasized that Ben called me to say that I'd gotten the Golden

Girl job, telling me in that intimate voice of his that I was beautiful, talented, and very smart—all the words my mother had used to describe me. But the fantasy didn't last long. It was so incredibly unrealistic that it kind of hurt to even imagine it. It would never happen to me in a million years.

I rolled over and turned on my radio. Well, I still couldn't wait for tomorrow, when I would answer the phone and actually get to speak to him again. I decided to concentrate on something good that really could happen.

He'd be calling to give me the bad news. He'd expect me to act disappointed, maybe even mad.

But I'll be such a good sport that he'll fall instantly in love with me and ask me out on a date, I thought, suddenly inspired.

I lay on my bed and practiced what I'd say. I was going to be really cool: "Oh, Ben, that's okay," I'd say. "Of course I understand! I'm in charge of poetry submissions at the literary magazine at school, so I'm pretty busy as it is. You wouldn't believe how much poetry everyone is writing at school these days!"

That cracked me up and I laughed out loud. *Come on, Claire. You call that cool?* I groaned and tried again.

"Of course, I wanted the job," I practiced out loud, "but Lana is so beautiful and so *very* talented."

I wondered if I could really say that without gagging. I sighed. Keeping Ben on the phone long enough to get asked out was going to be harder than I thought.

Audrey McCauley, my best friend, rushed up to me at school the next morning. I was standing at my locker pulling books off of the top shelf.

"How'd it go?" she asked. "Did you really go through with the audition?"

"Of course I did," I said. "I accepted the dare; I had no choice."

Audrey is a sophomore, too, and if you think *I'm* self-conscious, you should meet her. She's only about ten pounds overweight, but she calls herself The Blimp! She's really quite nice-looking, I think, with shoulder-length red hair, bright green eyes and incredibly straight teeth. Her parents sacrificed five years' worth of vacations to finance her mouth, but it really paid off.

"I have to tell you about it," I said. "I met the dreamiest guy in the world at that audition." I paused here and glanced over my shoulder to make sure that no one was listening. The hall was crowded, but everyone was headed toward a class or busy talking in groups. "And he is walking the halls somewhere in this hallowed institution as we speak!"

22

"More, more! Tell me more!" Audrey pressed in close to get more details. "What's his name?"

I leaned closer and lowered my voice. "His name is"—I hesitated a second before I spoke—"Ben Riley."

"Wow! Ben Riley!" she cried out, stepping back in surprise. "You *met* Ben Riley?"

"Keep quiet!" I whispered urgently, looking back over my shoulder again. No one seemed to notice the commotion we were making. Then I realized what she'd said. "Hold on a second. You know who he is?"

"Are you kidding?" she said. "I've known who he is since the first day of school! I saw him park his cute red convertible in the student parking lot, and then he parked his cute little derriere on the steps near the south lockers, and I couldn't believe he was for real. He looked like a movie star or something."

"Why didn't you tell me?" I asked.

"I *did* tell you!" she said. "I told you all about it!"

I stared at her a moment. She might have been right about that. She gets all worked up over a lot of boys at school and she tells me *in detail* about each and every one of them. It's impossible to keep all her stories straight.

"And guess who told me his name?" she asked. She hadn't intended for me to guess because she plowed right on. "Mary Jane and

I were getting off the bus on the first day. *She* told me who he was." Audrey rolled her eyes. "I knew if anyone would know his name, it'd be Mary Jane. She's *so* boy-crazy."

"Yeah, she sure is," I agreed.

"So tell me about him!" she said. "What's he like up close? Why was he there?"

"He was running the audition," I said. "His father is the executive producer and Ben's job was to choose the top five people."

"He *watched* you audition?" she asked, looking horrified.

"Yeah," I said. "Why?"

"Well, no offense," Audrey said, "but you were probably kind of awful, weren't you? I mean, you've never done that kind of thing before. I'd do a pretty lousy job, too."

"Well, thanks a lot. Have you forgotten that I played Ophelia once?" I asked defensively.

She stared at me a moment. "You mean that horrible speech you gave in the ninth grade? The one where you hiccuped after every other word?"

I was starting to get a bit irritated with Audrey.

"I wasn't all that bad," I said, crossing my arms over my chest.

"Well, okay," she said. "I suppose I could be just a teeny bit jealous about your having met Ben Riley and all." She suddenly looked worried. "What would I do if you suddenly got famous and started running around with Ben Riley's crowd?"

I put a hand on her arm. "You'd still be my very best friend," I said. "But it won't happen, so why are we even talking about it?"

"Right," she said. "Anyway, I'm sorry—tell me all about it."

"Well, I *was* terrific at the audition yesterday. Even Ben said so."

"Really?" I could see that she didn't believe me. "He actually used the word 'terrific'? And he wasn't being sarcastic?" Audrey bent down to grab some books.

"He was *very* sincere," I insisted, wishing I felt as convinced as I sounded. "He looked deep into my eyes and suggested that while I read the copy—that's the script—that I tempt him into going with me to the sale."

Audrey's mouth fell wide open. "You're kidding. He used the word '*tempt*'? I don't believe it. You're making this up."

"And do you know what he said at the very end?" I said. "He said, 'That was terrific,' and he lowered his voice and said in this very cozy tone, 'I'd follow you anywhere.' "

Audrey stood up abruptly. "Now I *know* you're making it up!" she said. "No boy on the face of the earth would say that. It's too sophisticated. He'd have to be at least twenty-three to pull off a line like that."

"I swear that's exactly what he said!" I said. "This guy is really sophisticated, Audrey. I know he's only seventeen, but he acts like a twenty-three-year-old."

"Well, maybe he's going to pick you as one of the top five."

"No way," I said. "I was good, but I was competing against Lana Boyson and her crowd. There are a lot more than five beautiful girls in that clique. And then think about all of the other girls at Lincoln High. And all the girls at North High—they auditioned last week. There are so many glamorous girls at that school I can't count them. So there's no way I'll be chosen. But, get this: Ben is going to call me tonight to tell me the results. I'm going to get to *talk* to him again!"

"What are you going to say?" Audrey asked.

"I'm going to be very nice, a little disappointed, but a great sport about the whole thing. And then I'm going to ask him out on a date for Saturday night."

"*No!*" she cried out, clapping a hand over her mouth.

I burst out laughing. "Of *course* I wouldn't ask Ben out!" I said. "I can't believe you fell for that, Audrey. I would never in a million years have the nerve to do that!"

Just then Audrey stood up very straight and looked over my shoulder. She shifted her eyes back to me without moving a muscle in her body. "Don't look now," she said, her mouth barely moving, "but he's heading this way at this very moment."

"Ben Riley?" I squealed.

"Umm-hmm," she said, a phony smile plastered on her face, her body stiff as a board.

"Act natural," I said, and I laughed in a way that I thought would come out sounding very melodious and charming, but instead came out very fake and forced. Audrey rolled her eyes.

Ben walked past me a short distance and stopped. He was soon surrounded by girls. They were all laughing at something he said. In fact, they all seemed to be trying to out-flirt each other, all the while giggling idiotically. It was the most sickening thing I'd ever seen.

He happened to glance in my direction then, and with a tiny movement of his head, nodded to me. Then he moved on, with the girls all following close behind him.

I turned back to Audrey, triumphant. "See?" I said. "He recognized me! He nodded to me."

"Oh, is that what it was?" she joked. "I thought he had a little nervous tic or something."

"Audrey, face the facts!" I cried out in exasperation. "I *met* him, he *knows* me, we're going to speak again on the phone tonight. If you can't be happy for me, don't bother pretending you're my friend."

"Okay, okay—keep your shirt on," Audrey said with a grin.

I smiled. "I'm sorry. I'm just so nervous about talking to him again."

"I don't blame you," she said. "Look at how these girls were hanging all over him. I wonder if he'll be as popular when he tells all but one of them that they weren't chosen."

"I'm sure he'll be really nice about it," I said. "Besides, a guy who looks like that doesn't ever lack for dates."

"You've got a point," Audrey agreed. "He's fantastically handsome."

"Do you think he lifts weights?" I asked. "He's got such an incredible body."

"He'd have to, with those muscles," she said. "When do you think he'll call?"

"Sometime tonight, he said." I leaned back against a locker and sighed. "I hope I don't get hit by a truck or something before I get a chance to answer the phone."

Audrey patted my shoulder. "Push that possibility right out of your mind," she said. "You'll talk to him. Just promise you'll call me right afterwards."

"I promise." Then I grinned. "And I'll tell you all about the plans for our hot date on Saturday night."

Audrey laughed. "You do that."

Chapter Three

I sat on the living room couch, checked the clock on the mantel, then returned to the short story I'd been assigned to read for English lit. It was eight o'clock and Ben still hadn't called. I'd been hovering close to the phone all evening, but it hadn't rung once.

Mom came in from the kitchen, sat down, and picked up the phone.

"Mom!" I cried. "What are you doing?"

Mom looked surprised. "I believe it's called making a telephone call. Why? What's the matter?"

"Will you be long?" I asked.

"No, I just want to get Marge's recipe for carrot juice. It's delicious!"

"Could you possibly wait and get it later tonight, or maybe even tomorrow? Ben's going to call about the results of the audition."

"No, honey, I'd like to make a batch tonight, if I have all of the ingredients. If he calls and I'm on the line, I'm sure he'll call right back."

She finished dialing and waited for her friend to answer.

"Hi, Marge, have you got time to give me that wonderful carrot juice recipe? Yes, that's the one. Sure, I'll hold on."

What if Ben is dialing my number right now? What if he gets a busy signal and then forgets to call me back?

I stood up and paced around the living room. I walked to the window and drew aside the drape and stared out into the darkness.

"Okay," Mom said, "yes, I have a pencil. Go ahead."

I walked over to the mantel clock and stared at it pointedly. Mom didn't see me, though. She was too busy writing down ingredients. I cleared my throat and tapped my fingernails against the mantel. Still she didn't look up.

I flopped down on the couch and sighed as loudly as I could. Mom looked up and frowned at me and went back to her note-taking.

Then I formed the "time out" signal with my hands, right under her nose.

She looked up and rolled her eyes, nodded and mouthed the words *I know.*

"Okay, Marge," she said. "Thanks a lot. I'm going to have to get off the phone so that it's clear for my daughter. That's right; wait till your kids are teenagers." She laughed. "Okay, I'll talk to you soon. 'Bye."

I couldn't believe it when she finally hung up.

"*There*, I'm finished," she said. "Can you relax now?"

I collapsed onto the couch and groaned. "No, not until Ben calls."

Dad walked into the room then, puffing on his pipe, and sat in his favorite easy chair, next to the fireplace, to read the evening paper.

This seemed to be a good time to discuss something that had been weighing on my mind. I'd been worrying that when Ben called they'd hang around to listen to my side of the conversation, making me feel very self-conscious.

I cleared my throat.

"Can I talk to you guys?" I asked.

"Sure," Mom said. "Tom, Claire wants to talk to us."

"Okay," Dad said without removing the pipe from his mouth. "Shoot."

"Well, when Ben Riley calls tonight, he'll have the results of the Golden Girl contest. Now, of course, I won't get the job— "

"You don't know that," Mom interrupted. "Dad and I agree that you're the best girl for the job." She waved at Dad to get his attention. "Don't we, Tom?"

"Sure," he said, blowing little puffs of smoke

31

toward the ceiling. Dad's a man of few words. He's an accountant, and I think he feels more comfortable with numbers and tax forms than with people.

I gazed at them, first my mother, then my father. "Well, seeing as how neither of you auditioned any of the applicants—and considering the fact that you're my parents and slightly prejudiced—I think your opinion doesn't count for much. No offense. But thanks for the support, anyway."

"You're welcome, dear," Mom said, smiling.

"Anyway, when the phone rings, I'd kind of like to have some privacy during the call, okay? Because I want to make a good impression and be a good sport and say all the right things, but if you're listening to what I'm saying, I'll get nervous and self-conscious and stutter and stammer and talk in circles and—"

"Sort of like you are now?" Dad asked, squinting through the haze of smoke in front of his face.

"Well, yes, I guess so," I said. "So you'll let me get the phone and then stay out of the way for a few minutes?"

"Sure, no problem," Mom said. "It's important for you to have your privacy."

"Thanks," I said, totally relieved.

But by ten-thirty Ben still hadn't called. I went upstairs, grabbed my pillow and a blanket, and dragged them downstairs to continue the wait.

"What are you doing?" Mom asked.

"Waiting for the phone to ring," I said. I fluffed the pillow and spread out the blanket on the couch.

"You're going to sleep down here?" Mom said.

"Yeah. That's okay, isn't it? I don't want to miss Ben's call."

"Honey, he probably isn't going to call tonight. It's too late. He'll probably talk to you at school tomorrow."

"I can't take the chance of missing his call," I said. "He said he'd call tonight. There's no reason why he shouldn't."

"Okay," Mom said, shrugging. She blew me a kiss and headed upstairs to bed.

I crawled under the blanket on the couch and got situated, making sure that I could reach the phone easily from my "bed." I turned out the light and stared up at the ceiling.

The telephone remained quiet.

Ben probably didn't want to bother making the phone calls to tell girls who hadn't been picked. Maybe he'd decided to call only the girl who was chosen. Suddenly, I had a horrible thought. What if he'd decided to announce the chosen girl at school and not call anyone at all? Surely that would make more sense and save him many hours on the phone.

I groaned, rolled over, and punched my pillow. Maybe I would never talk to him again. Then I wouldn't have a chance to impress him with my good-sport routine and he'd never fall madly in love with me. I pulled the pillow over my head and, after another half hour of anguish, felt myself begin to drift off. *I guess I'll just have to face the fact that my relationship with Ben was just a fantasy I've had since four o'clock yesterday*, I thought before falling asleep.

Audrey was waiting for me at my locker when I got to school the next day.

She looked at me, her eyes filled with sympathy. "How are you doing, kid?" she asked. as she put an arm around my shoulders.

I spun the combination dial on my locker. "Fine, other than a little headache," I said. "Why?"

"Well, I figured when you didn't call last night that you were so depressed after talking to Ben that you couldn't bring yourself to talk to me. But remember, Claire, I'm your friend through thick and thin. If you want to pour your heart out to me and tell me how lousy you feel and how humiliating it was to accept the bad news, I'd be glad to listen."

"Thanks, Audrey," I said, opening the door to my locker, "but he didn't call."

"He couldn't break the news," Audrey said,

nodding sadly. "He didn't want to hurt you because he knew how much you wanted the job." She sighed. "What a nice guy."

I picked up my geometry textbook, closed the door, and turned to face Audrey. "Did it occur to you that maybe the decision hasn't been made yet?"

She glanced at me sadly. "Sure, sure," she said, patting my arm. "Maybe that's it."

I rolled my eyes. "Audrey, don't waste your pity on me. I know that I won't be chosen, but I'll still get to talk to him. I'm sure he'll call tonight."

"I'm sure he will," she said.

The bell rang then, and she gave my arm one last sympathetic squeeze and ran off.

I looked for Ben all day in the halls but didn't see him until just before my last class. I was standing outside my science classroom when he came striding in my direction. I decided to speak. Maybe he'd explain why he hadn't called last night.

"Hi, Ben," I called out and waved.

He looked over, held a hand up in greeting, and passed right by. No smile, no hello, nothing. He didn't even slow down.

The weak side of me felt crushed. I wanted to run into the bathroom and cry my eyes out. But the strong side of me was angry. I wanted to tear his head off for being unfriendly after I'd made him the object of my fantasies for nearly two days. Both emotions were completely irrational and pulled me in two separate directions, but that's the way I felt.

And then Joe's comment came back to me. Maybe Ben *did* tell all the girls who auditioned that they were "terrific." Maybe he even told all of them that he'd follow them anywhere.

I felt sick. How could I have been so stupid as to think that I had even a *tiny* chance of getting Ben to like me?

I decided that I didn't care whether he called me. In fact, I felt a little relieved that I wouldn't have to sweat out another night waiting for him to call. *Yes, I decided, this is a healthier attitude. I don't care about Ben Riley one way or the other. He's cute, but I can live without him.*

The day seemed to drag on forever. After school I had a meeting with the literary magazine staff, but I couldn't concentrate and hardly heard a word that was said. I was glad I'd decided to forget about Ben, but it would take a little time before I felt really great about my decision. For now, I couldn't help feeling depressed.

I walked home from school and dragged myself up the porch steps. The phone was ringing as I walked in the front door.

"Will somebody get that?" I hollered, throwing my books on the front table.

"How about *you*, since you're out there?" Mom called from the kitchen. "I'm taking something out of the oven."

I sighed deeply and crossed the living room to the phone next to the couch.

"Hello?" I said gruffly.

"Hi, Claire," a voice said. "This is Ben Riley."

Suddenly, all my feelings came rushing back with a vengeance. I cared a whole lot about Ben Riley, that was obvious. My depression suddenly vanished and I felt alert and energetic. *I was talking to Ben Riley!* My stomach flipped over and my heart started hammering away in my chest. Funny what one phone call can do.

"I'm sorry I didn't call you last night," he said, "but the final decision about the Golden Girl wasn't made until very late this afternoon."

Be a good sport, be a good sport, I kept repeating to myself.

"Oh, that's okay, Ben," I said, concentrating so hard I could hardly hear him. "No problem. None at all."

Be a good sport. Remember your speech.

"I want to be the first to congratulate you," he said. "You're our new Golden Girl!"

"Oh, that's okay, Ben," I said. "Lana is so beautiful and so very—" Then I caught myself. "Um, what did you say?"

He laughed. It was a wonderful, incredible sound. Then he spoke in that soft, intimate voice. "You, Claire Montgomery, are the new Golden Girl." He paused. "How do you feel?"

"I—I—can't believe it," I said. "I don't know what to say." I was being perfectly honest. I was prepared to lose, but I certainly wasn't prepared to *win*! It just couldn't be true. "You're *sure*?"

Ben laughed. "We're going to have to do something about your self-confidence," he said. "Your audition was wonderful."

My audition was wonderful?

"But how did it happen?" I asked. "I mean, what did they like about me? What did I do right?"

Ben laughed again. "That's what they liked —the honesty, the unpretentiousness of your performance. And you showed a lot of spunk by adding that extra line at the end. I think that's what finally put you ahead of the others. They really liked you, Claire."

And what about you, Ben Riley? You thought my audition was wonderful, but did you like me?

"This has to be the best phone call I've ever gotten," I said. "Thank you, Ben."

He softened his voice even more. "It was my pleasure." Then he chuckled. "That's another rough thing about this job, telling a girl she's going to be a star."

I laughed. *Me, a star?*

"Actually, this is the only good part of my

job tonight," he said. "I'm kind of dreading all the rest of the calls. I mean, to the girls who *weren't* chosen. I guess I'm not going to be the most popular guy at school tomorrow."

I didn't know how to answer that. I realized that it probably would be hard to tell all the girls who'd dreamed for years of getting the Golden Girl job. And maybe they *would* hold it against him.

"We're going to make some small changes in your hair and makeup," he said, changing the subject. "I'll talk to you about that later."

Cut off all my hair. Paint my face bright blue. Your wish is my command.

"Okay," I said, "if you think it's necessary."

"So, I guess that's all for now," he said. "See you at school tomorrow. And congratulations again."

"Thanks, Ben. 'Bye." I calmly put down the phone and walked into the kitchen, where Mom, Dad, and Joe were starting dinner.

"I won! I won! I won!" I screamed, jumping up and down. I whooped and hollered and danced in a circle while my family looked on in astonishment. Finally I collapsed in my chair at the table, breathing heavily, with a big, stupid grin on my face.

My brother looked up from his plate. "Pass the mashed potatoes, will you, Mom?" he said.

My mouth fell open, but Mom laughed, got

up from her chair, and came around to hug me.

"Congratulations!" she said. "You deserve it! But I'm not surprised, darling. You're a very talented young lady. They just used good, common sense in selecting you. Didn't they, Tom?"

"Sure did," my father said.

"Yeah," Joe said. "Way to go, Care." He looked up at Mom. "So will you pass the mashed potatoes now?"

"There you go, Joe," I said. I shoved the bowl of potatoes across the table toward my brother. Suddenly Joe was alert, as he grabbed the bowl before it fell in his lap. I could afford to be a little wild tonight. It wasn't every day that I was chosen from all the girls in the city to be Trent's Golden Girl! The job was enough, but I was going to be working closely—as closely as I could possibly manage it—with the most amazing guy in the world!

I ran directly to Audrey's house right after dinner. She only lived three blocks away, and the news was too good to deliver over the phone.

"They chose *you*?" she asked. "Really?" She paused, then looked at me with a suspicious glint in her eye. "You don't think he's playing a mean trick on you, do you?"

I sighed. "I know it's hard to believe. I thought he'd made a mistake, too. But apparently they really liked me and chose me for the job."

"This isn't just a job," Audrey pointed out seriously. "This is the chance of a lifetime, the kind of opportunity every girl dreams of. Glitz, glamour, and guys. The three G's. Not to mention big bucks."

"Not so big," I said. "Minimum wage."

"For the three G's, I'd do it for nothing," she said. Then her face brightened. "And just think, I'm your best friend. Think some of the benefits might rub off on me?"

I shrugged. "Why not? Hitch yourself to a rising star."

"Not too modest, are you?" she said, and we both laughed. "But seriously, Claire, think who you'll be working with, week in and week out. I think I'd die of happiness right now if I were you." She stopped abruptly. "Will you introduce me to Ben?"

"Of course," I said, though I was starting to feel just a bit possessive.

"Oh, I'm so glad you got this job!" she said. "It's going to be so exciting!"

"It certainly is!" I agreed with a happy laugh.

My brother actually offered me a ride to school the next day. And not only that—he put his arm around me, and we walked into school together and down the hall to my locker. I thought I was going to faint—he'd never paid so much attention to me in my life.

"Hey, Claire, I hear you're the new Golden Girl!" one of Joe's friends shouted. Joe gave my shoulder an affectionate squeeze and waved back. I'd never seen Joe look so proud.

"Claire, way to go!" a girl from my math class called out.

"Here comes our newest star!" someone else shouted.

A couple of cute guys from the swim team approached and Joe introduced them to me. They smiled and congratulated me, and then some more of his friends came up to meet me.

My head was spinning. I was an instant celebrity, and I won't lie: It felt great!

"Claire, sit with me at lunch?" someone called out.

"Claire, want to go to the basketball game with a bunch of us this weekend?"

"Claire, there's a party on Saturday night at my house. You've *got* to come!" said a pretty blond girl from my science class.

All of this happened before homeroom. I didn't really know what to think or how to handle all of the attention. Nothing like this had ever happened to me before.

"Uh, I'm going to the rest room to fix my hair," I whispered to Joe. "See you later."

I retreated to the girls' room and closed myself up in one of the stalls. It was good to be by myself for a few minutes after all that attention. I heard the rest room door open and the sound of feet shuffling in.

"Why would they pick *her*?" a voice asked. "She's not even a junior and she's certainly nowhere near as pretty as you are!"

"She's not as pretty as half the girls who tried out," a familiar voice said.

"Lana, I don't know how Claire Montgomery stole the Golden Girl job away from you, but somehow she managed to do it. It's unbelievable!"

I felt my whole body stiffen and my stomach suddenly got sour. I *stole* the Golden Girl job? What did they mean by that?

I decided to stay in the stall until those obnoxious girls left. I sure wasn't going to walk out now, right into the middle of the lions' den.

Then I heard Lana's voice again. "That's just it. I could take it if she were superpretty or talented or seemed to have the qualities that a Golden Girl should have. But she's so blah! Have you seen her?" Mumbled voices indicated yes. "She's okay-looking, and thin, but she's so flat-chested! What in the world did Ben see in her, anyway?"

Blah? Flat-chested? I was beginning to get

pretty angry. How dare they stand there and criticize me so viciously!

"Well, I didn't get the Golden Girl job," Lana continued. "But I'm not going to stand by and let her get her hands on Ben Riley. I've had my eye on him for three years, and I'm not giving up on him without a battle! She'd better watch out if she knows what's good for her." The other girls laughed appreciatively.

I clenched my hands into fists and had to restrain myself from running out of the stall and punching her out. No one threatens Claire Montgomery and gets away with it.

"Who *knows* why they chose her!" said one of the other voices. "Maybe her parents have pull with Mr. Trent or Ben's parents. Maybe they belong to the same country club and play golf together or something like that. Maybe they were owed a big favor. . . ."

Without even thinking about it, I burst out of the stall and strode right up to Lana. "You can insult *me*, Lana Boyson," I yelled in her face. "I can take it from you and your moron friends, but never insult my parents again! I won't take that from you or *anybody!*"

Lana just stood there, stunned, her mouth hanging open. Then she collected herself and mumbled, "Come on, girls," and slid out of the rest room.

I waited a full three minutes to give them plenty of time to leave the hallway. Then I scurried out of the rest room so I wouldn't be late for my first class.

And all the way down the hallway I noticed that everyone was staring at me. But now I didn't feel like a celebrity or a magazine cover girl. This time I felt like one of the freaks featured on the front page of the *National Enquirer*: "Ugliest Girl in the Midwest Wins Rigged Beauty Pageant."

I wanted to die. Were all the kids who pointed at me wondering how I'd managed to land the Golden Girl job? Did they think I was a flat-chested blah person, too?

There was a hard lump in my throat that ached like nothing I'd ever felt before. It hurt all morning, even as everyone continued to congratulate me on winning the Golden Girl job. I didn't even feel like talking to anyone.

I somehow got through lunch with all the girls at the table pelting me with questions about my new job. Would I tape a commercial every other week or would I tape two commercials at a time? Would I be able to choose what I wore on TV? Would Trent's provide my clothes free? Did I think the job would be hard? Did I feel like a celebrity? One question they asked over and over: Would Ben Riley be working with me all year, and what *exactly* would his duties be?

Unfortunately, I couldn't answer most of their questions, but they didn't seem to mind.

They just chattered on and on about how lucky I was and how my life was going to change drastically.

Audrey kept looking at me strangely, but she was quiet during most of the meal.

After lunch, she pushed me into a corner in the hall and said, "Okay, what gives?"

"What do you mean?" I asked.

"Something's wrong," she said. "I know you and I know when you're deliriously happy, as you should be at this moment. But you're not, Claire Montgomery, you're faking it. So what happened? I'm your best friend and I deserve to know."

"Wow," I said, taking a step back and looking at her admiringly. "You really are perceptive."

"Not really," she said, "it's just that even though you got the Golden Girl job, you're a crummy actress!"

So I told her about the incident in the rest room. When I'd finished relating what I'd heard through the bathroom stall door, she whistled.

"Boy, are you in for it now!" she said.

"What do you mean, I'm 'in for it'? I'm not scared of those girls."

"Lana's going to come after you." She thought a minute. "Do you think you'll end up in a cat fight, rolling around on the floor with her, like they do in soap operas?"

"Are you kidding?" I asked. "That's ridiculous."

"But what if she comes after you?"

"Will you cut it out?" I cried. "Lana may have Jell-O between her ears, but she's got some class. Besides, when she said she wasn't giving Ben up without a battle, she didn't mean it *literally*."

Audrey gazed at me with those big green eyes. "I hope for your sake that you're right."

Suddenly she grabbed my arm. "Don't look now but here he comes!" she whispered. "Ben Riley! He's coming this way, and he's lookin' good!"

"How far away?" I asked, staring down at my feet.

She lowered her head so as not to look at him and whispered, "Less than halfway down the hall. I think he saw you." She touched my arm. "Tell me, am I drooling?"

"All over your sweater," I mumbled. "Act natural. He's going to wonder what's so interesting on the floor."

"Natural, right." She cleared her throat and raised her head. "So what were your New Year's resolutions, Claire?" she asked in a loud, enthusiastic voice.

I rolled my eyes and shook my head.

"Too phony?" she whispered.

"Yeah," I said. Just then I felt a warm hand

47

on my shoulder, and I whirled around. "Oh, hi!" I said.

"Hi yourself," said Ben, smiling warmly.

He looked as if he'd stepped out of the pages of *Gentleman's Quarterly*. He was wearing a loose white shirt and stylish, slightly baggy black pants and black loafers.

If I'm dreaming, don't wake me up. If I've died, don't resuscitate me. Life doesn't get any better than this.

"Remember when we were talking about a makeover for you?" Ben asked. He held up a fashion magazine and opened it to a picture of a girl about my age with a pretty, wavy hairstyle.

"I want you to take this picture with you when you have your hair done. Bernie at Hair Creations is going to give you a similar hairstyle. Okay?"

I nodded.

"I've already talked to her," Ben continued. "I think you'll look really great with your hair like this. See? Your face has the same shape and your hair is fine and full like the model's."

He reached out and traced the side of my face from my temple to my chin with his finger.

Life just improved about five hundred percent, I thought, amazed by what his touch had made me feel.

I caught a glimpse of Audrey out of the

corner of my eye. If I hadn't been in a dream-like state myself, I would've laughed out loud. Her mouth was open and her eyes were bugging out of her head, as if she couldn't believe what she was seeing.

Ben turned to Audrey and nodded his head toward me. "She's the perfect Golden Girl, don't you think?"

Audrey, still staring, didn't move. What in the world was wrong with her? I gave her a little kick.

"OH, YES!" she exclaimed in a voice loud enough for the whole hall to hear. "She's absolutely perrrr-fect!"

I stared at Audrey, mortified.

"Are you okay?" Ben asked Audrey seriously.

"Oh, yes," I said casually, "she's fine." I glanced at Audrey. "I think."

"Well, I need to get to class," Ben said. "Can you meet me at Trent's tonight? I want to take you shopping for some clothes for our first TV spot. How about seven, at the entrance near the fountain?"

"Yes, right. I know where you mean," I said. "I'll be there."

"Great," he said, smiling. "See you later, Golden Girl."

"Yeah, right. Great." I smiled and sort of waved as he walked off.

Audrey fell back against the lockers behind her and clutched her throat. "I thought I was going to die with him so nearby," she said. "It should be a crime to look that good."

"Yeah, but he does," I pointed out.

"And he touched your face," she said. "You are so lucky to be working with him, Claire. This is unreal. And he's going to buy you clothes and have you change your hair, just like something out of *My Fair Lady*. He's going to transform you from a wretched, filthy street girl into the belle of the ball."

I elbowed her—hard. " 'A wretched, filthy street girl'?! Give me a break, Audrey, I'm not *that* bad."

Audrey giggled. "It's just so romantic!" she exclaimed.

Just then, someone tapped me on the shoulder. I whirled around, expecting it to be Ben again. But it was Lana Boyson, ready for another stab at ruining my day.

"What's the matter, Lana?" I asked, still angry from this morning. "Think up some new insults?" I pretended to check my watch. "Gee, and it only took you seven hours to come up with them!"

Lana scowled. "There's something I just thought you ought to know," she said. "I wouldn't count on getting cozy with Ben Riley."

"Oh, that's right," I said sarcastically. "You have Ben Riley targeted for yourself. I heard you tell your plans to your buddies earlier today. Remember?"

"I admit I'm interested in Ben," she said. "But it doesn't look like either of us is going to get him. He's already got a serious girlfriend."

I couldn't help it. I wasn't prepared for the news, and my face must have fallen to the floor.

Lana smiled smugly. "She's a student at North High. She's rich, talented, and"—she swept her eyes over me with obvious disdain—"very, very cute."

Chapter Four

Although I was still a bit perturbed by Lana's remark, I called Bernie at Hair Creations right after school. She said she had an opening at five o'clock if I wanted to take it. I figured that I might as well make the change in my hair right away. That would show Ben and his dad that I was taking the Golden Girl job seriously. And anyway, that was obviously how I was going to have to keep my relationship with Ben, like it or not: purely professional. After all, according to Lana, Ben was already taken.

I was very nervous when I walked into Hair Creations at five, though, carrying the magazine that Ben had given me. I'd had my hair cut a few times at beauty salons, but usually my mom just trimmed the ends for me at home. I wished Audrey could have been there with me, but she'd promised to help her mother with some errands.

I waited at the reception desk, and looked around the sleek shop. There were eight stations at various places in the room, each having a chair, counter, and mirror. Five of them were now occupied with hairdressers and their clients. The shop had a lot of long windows and a line of skylights overhead, and there were green plants hanging from the ceiling and tucked into every conceivable corner. The place had a big, airy quality, in spite of the smell of chemicals that filled the room.

A small, dark-haired woman approached me. "May I help you?" she asked. She wore a name tag that read BERNIE.

"Hi," I said. "I'm Claire Montgomery. I'm your five o'clock appointment."

She brightened. "So you're the new Golden Girl. I talked with Ben Riley yesterday, and he told me all about you."

I handed her the magazine. "Ben said I should ask for a style similar to this one." I watched her face for her reaction. She studied the picture and then looked up at me and back at the picture. "Do you think you can make me look like this?"

"Yes, I think you'll look quite attractive in this style," she said, nodding her approval.

"Boy, I hope you're right. I don't want to be the laughingstock of Lincoln High."

She patted my hand, laughing, and led me to a chair next to a sink. She washed my hair, toweled it off, and then had me move to her station, where she combed out my hair.

Ordinarily, I love going to the beauty salon and having someone work on my hair. It's so luxurious just sitting there while someone gently washes and styles it.

But today I was very nervous. I was afraid that I'd made a big mistake by allowing Ben to have so much control over my appearance. What if he was wrong about the new style and I looked awful? What if Bernie made a big mistake and my hair came out looking lopsided or something?

If that happens, I decided, *I just won't go to school tomorrow.* I'd suddenly get a sore throat and stay home in bed while I figured out how I could convince my family to move to a different town.

Bernie trimmed about two inches off the ends of my hair and layered the rest around my face. I kept a close watch, but it didn't look like she was doing anything very radical.

Then she got out her plastic perm rods and rolled them tightly into my hair. She squirted a smelly solution onto them and had me sit under the drier. While the warm air blew on my head, I read *Seventeen* magazine and studied the models on every page. Their hair, makeup, and clothes interested me much more than they usually did, because of my new job. They were all so beautiful and poised. It was interesting but incredibly depressing at the same time—a whole magazine filled with Lana Boyson clones!

"Yuck," I said, and tossed the magazine on the table next to me.

Bernie came back then and took me to the sink. She put some more stuff on my hair, waited five minutes, then rinsed it again and toweled it off. After I spent another twenty minutes under the drier, she took me to her chair again.

I looked at myself in the mirror for the first time. The perm made it look as if I had suddenly sprouted twice as much hair.

Bernie combed my hair out, using a hair pick. She stepped back a bit and looked at me in the mirror.

"I think I'll use the curling iron on you," she said. "That'll tone down the frizziness of the new perm and create big waves."

I watched her take sections of my hair and roll them up in the warm iron. It took about ten minutes. Then she carefully combed it out.

"*Voilà!*" she said, standing back to admire her work. "My goodness, Ben Riley was right, wasn't he? This hairstyle really suits your face well."

I couldn't believe how different I looked! I

never would've known that my lackluster hair could be so full and look so glamorous.

"You see," Bernie said, "this style helps to give your face some definition." She smiled warmly. "You have lovely eyes, dear. Shorter hair emphasizes your features."

I'm sure my blushing revealed that I wasn't accustomed to compliments. Mothers don't count.

"Thank you," I said, hurriedly. "You do good work. Uh, do you have a curling iron that I could buy from you?" I asked.

"Surely," Bernie said as she led the way to the receptionist's desk.

I paid her for the curling iron and put on my coat. Bernie told me that the salon had donated its services for the contest. She followed me to the door.

"You like the new style?"

"Oh, yes, I love it!" I said. "I can't believe it's me!"

"It's you, all right." She grinned. "I hope Ben Riley is ready to see his new Golden Girl. I think he's going to be very pleased."

"Thanks," I said.

She waved as I opened the door. "See you on TV!" she called after me.

I hopped on the bus and rode it directly to the mall to meet Ben. It was a good thing I'd told Mom I wouldn't have time to get home for dinner. Who could eat at a time like this, anyway? I was so nervous about meeting him!

I hurried to the mall's rest room and combed my hair. The wind had blown it around, so it didn't look as perfect as it had in the salon, but it still looked good. I just hoped Ben thought so.

I found him sitting on the edge of the fountain right outside of Trent's Department Store. When he saw me, he looked confused for a moment, then stood up and broke into a big grin.

"What did I tell you?" he said, standing back to get a better look at me. "Turn around."

I slowly turned in front of him and he nodded. "You look great."

My blush for Bernie was just a warm-up for what my face did then. I mean, we're talking fire-engine red. I tried to sound cool. "Hey, thanks," I said.

Ben laughed. "It'd be fun to follow you around at school tomorrow and see all the heads turn when you walk by."

I laughed and rolled my eyes. "Oh, right."

"No, I'm not kidding," Ben said. "I can think of a couple of girls who are going to be really upset."

"You couldn't possibly be referring to Lana Boyson, could you?" I asked, smiling.

"Lana Boyson? Jealous?" Ben said, his grin widening.

I threw back my head and laughed. Ben reached out and tugged playfully at a strand of my hair.

"I guess if I want to become a director, I have to get used to working with all kinds of people," Ben said. "No matter how weird they are."

"Are you still talking about Lana Boyson?" I asked.

"No, I'm talking about *you*," he teased.

"Who, *moi*?" I said, grinning. "You've got to be kidding."

"Come on," he said, guiding me into Trent's. "Let's talk to Betty. She'll decide whether you're weird or not. Be prepared," he warned. "She always agrees with me."

He led me to the cosmetics department and signaled the saleswoman behind the counter. She was about thirty, dark-haired, and very attractive. She beamed when she saw Ben. "Why, Ben, I haven't seen you in a long time," she said. "You used to come in all the time with your dad and Mr. Trent." Then she got a sly glint in her eye and said, "My, how you've *grown*. And I see you've got a new girlfriend. How does your old girlfriend, Jennifer, feel about this?"

My stomach flipped over when she said that, and I glanced up at Ben. He seemed as surprised as I was that Betty had mentioned Jennifer.

There was a long, awkward pause and he

laughed a little nervously. "Jennifer's fine," he said. "Uh, Betty, this is Trent's new Golden Girl, Claire Montgomery. I thought you might work with her a little. You know, choose the right colors for her and show her how to emphasize her eyes. We want her to look her best for the camera."

"Oh, sure," she said, smiling, "I'd be glad to."

"I think I'll take a look around," Ben said, taking a step backward, looking very uncomfortable. "I'll be back in a little while."

"Okay," I said in a soft voice, watching him hurry away.

Why did Betty have to mention Jennifer and ruin everything? His girlfriend was the last person on earth I wanted to think about now.

Betty turned back to me. "That kid gets better-looking every time I see him."

"Tell me about it," I said.

She sighed. "If only I were fifteen years younger."

Even older women are attracted to Ben! I thought.

"I think I embarrassed him a little, asking him about his girlfriend." She chuckled a little. "Teenagers." Then she turned to me. "Now," she said, smiling, "let's see what we can do for you."

I wasn't really in the mood for a makeover

now, but I didn't exactly have a choice. I listened dejectedly to Betty as she told me how to apply the blush, eyeliner, and mascara so that my eyes became the focal point of my face. After a half hour of listening to Betty and trying several shades of base, eye shadow, lipstick, and mascara, I looked in the mirror on the counter at the final results.

"Wow, I look fantastic!" I blurted out, then covered my mouth with my hand.

Betty laughed and clapped her hands. "What a nice response," she said. "Most women would think they'd be boasting to say something like that. But since I'm the one who helped you to create the effect, I really like to hear that!" She paused and studied our work, just like a painter evaluating her canvas. "Yes," she said, "you really do look wonderful."

I sure did look different. It's amazing what a good hairstyle and makeup can do to emphasize your best features. My eyes looked sparkling and dramatic, but not overdone.

"Think you'll remember what we just did so you can apply your makeup before you shoot the commercials?" Betty asked.

"I think so," I said. "Thanks, Betty, for all the time you gave me. I really appreciate it."

Betty shrugged and smiled. "Hey, I'm just doing my job!"

I looked over my shoulder. "I wonder where Ben is," I said.

As soon as I spoke, I caught sight of him walking toward me out of the young men's department. He approached me, a little stiffly, I thought, and smiled. "Yes, that's good," he said. "Betty, you did a nice job here."

"Nice?" I blurted out, then grinned. "Not sensational or even glamorous?"

He nodded, as if he hadn't heard me. "That's just what we're looking for."

Betty smiled. "Good, I'm glad you like it," she said. "I think Claire looks beautiful."

Ben nodded but didn't say anything.

So speak up. Say something nice.

"Thanks again, Betty," I mumbled, barely able to contain my disappointment.

"Ready to get some clothes for our first shoot, Claire?" Ben asked. "By the way, you'll need to be available the day after tomorrow in the evening to tape the first two spots. Mr. Trent wants to get some commercials on the air right away."

"Oh, sure," I said, watching his face for a trace of the warmth that he'd shown me before Betty made the comment about Jennifer. There was no real friendliness there now, just courtesy. That gnawing pain in my chest that I'd felt earlier in the day was back.

Is this what a broken heart feels like? I wondered. Then I scolded myself. *How could you have a broken heart? You hardly know this guy. You only met him a few days ago.*

Joe had told me that Ben was just a guy like any other. I had to remember that!

I waved goodbye to Betty as we started over to the junior department.

"I think you should wear a dress for the first spot," Ben said.

The junior area was crowded with racks of blue jeans, sweaters, skirts, blouses, and a few spring items that must have just come in. Ben walked toward the far wall, where there were rows of dresses.

He snapped his fingers and pointed to a deep rose-colored dress hanging near the fitting rooms.

"That's good," he said. "Try this one on."

I was startled. "Really?" I would never have chosen it for myself, but I wasn't sure why. The dress was made of a light, flimsy fabric—not at all my type of thing.

I looked through the dresses on that rack, found a size 7, and took it down.

"Come out when you have it on," Ben said.

"Anything you say, *sir*," I said, totally irritated. Where was all of that charm Ben was so famous for? His helpful hints were beginning to sound like orders. If this kept up, I would soon have to ask Ben to stop treating me like a puppet.

I took the dress into a fitting room, took off my jeans and blouse, and pulled the dress over my head.

"Wow," I breathed when I'd gotten it on. It was beautiful! I stared at my reflection in the mirror and turned one way, then the other, watching the dress swing gracefully. The fabric draped over my body very nicely. It clung a bit to my waist, which is pretty small, and made my figure look its best. I felt so beautiful, so feminine, so—unlike anything I'd ever felt before.

"Claire?" Ben's voice startled me.

I'd forgotten about Ben standing outside the dressing room, waiting to see how I looked. I laughed and fluffed my hair and walked out to meet Ben. He was standing self-consciously over by the wall, probably feeling out of place in a girls' department.

I watched his eyes sweep over me and pause near my feet. His mouth dropped open and he frowned slightly. I looked down to where he was staring.

Suddenly I gasped. I'd left my red-and-white athletic socks on! And if that wasn't bad enough, there was a big hole in the right toe! How could I have overlooked the socks? I guess I was so overwhelmed by the beautiful dress that I just didn't look below my knees.

"Like 'em?" I said, smiling and wiggling my big toe. Actually, I wanted to crawl into a hole somewhere and hibernate for the rest of the winter, but I didn't want Ben to notice my embarrassment. I did a little dance and ended it with a curtsy, holding the dress up a little above my knees.

Ben tried not to smile, but he couldn't quite pull it off. "Great," he said. "Maybe you could wear those socks when we do the commercial and we'll start with a close-up of your big toe." Then his smile widened. "Be sure to paint your toenail bright red to match the socks."

"You have an artist's mind!" I said. "Great idea!"

We both laughed then and he shook his head. "The dress is great. Take it off and I'll arrange to borrow it for the shoot."

"Sure thing," I said.

Ben made the arrangements with the salesperson while I changed, and he walked me back toward the fountain entrance.

"Well, thanks for meeting me here," he said. "I think we're about ready for the first shoot." He grinned. "I'm really looking forward to that. Dad and Mr. Trent will be there and I'll get my first real experience working on a commercial. It should be fun."

"Good," I said. "I'm looking forward to it, too." *But for different reasons, Ben Riley.*

He handed me a slip of paper that read Friday, 7 P.M., KIRQ-TV.

"That's the time and the place," he said. "Can you make it?"

"Of course," I said. "No problem."

He grinned. "I can see you're a real professional. I knew you would be. See you later." He waved, and walked toward the mall entrance. I wanted to run after him, and talk to him a few more minutes, but I held back. I'd have plenty of time to talk to him on Friday. If he came to the shoot on Friday, at least I'd know he wasn't with Jennifer.

I didn't know what he thought about *me*, but at least he thought my attitude was professional. I wanted to make him glad that he and his father had chosen me. If I couldn't be his girlfriend, at least I could have his respect and friendship.

I looked at my watch. It wasn't quite eight o'clock. I'd brought along $75 of my birthday money thinking that I might have to pay for the salon visit. Now that I had all this extra money, why not buy a new outfit to wear to school tomorrow to go with my new hairstyle and makeup?

I don't need Ben Riley for a boyfriend, I thought. *There are plenty of other fish at Lincoln High!*

I found a stylish skirt-and-sweater outfit on sale, in the same deep rose color as the dress, and I paid for it with my birthday money. I still had $20 left over, and had an idea about how to spend it, but I wasn't sure I had the nerve to go through with it.

Finally, I gathered up my courage and took

the escalator up to the lingerie department. I'd never bought underwear without my mother along, and I was nervous. But I figured that at fifteen, it was about time I bought a bra by myself. I looked at the bras on display, though I wasn't really sure what I was looking for.

Then a white-haired woman dressed in a red suit approached me. "Can you find your size?" she asked.

"Um, well, yes, but—" I hesitated, not sure how to say it. "Well, I'm looking for something that could maybe, well, *help* me a little to, you know, look a little more . . ." I hurried on, afraid she'd get the wrong idea. "I mean, I don't want something that'll look as if I stuck socks in my bra or anything like that, I just want to improve on what I've got." I blushed and looked at her. "Do you know what I mean?"

She nodded and smiled just a tiny bit. "I think I know exactly what you need," she said thoughtfully. She led me to a rack.

"These bras have an underwire and a small amount of padding. I think you'll like them."

"Wire?" I asked. "Don't they hurt after a while?"

"Oh, no," she said cheerfully. "I wear them all the time, and they're very comfortable. They enhance what nature has given you."

I took two different styles back to the dressing room and tried them on. One was horrible; it made me look puffed-out in front. But the other one looked great. I put my blouse on over it, and there really *was* an improvement!

After I was dressed again, I paid for the bra and took a bus home. I couldn't wait for tomorrow! The kids at Lincoln High were going to see me with my great new hairstyle, makeup, and clothes! I could almost hear the trumpet fanfare announcing my arrival at school.

Introducing the new Claire Montgomery!

Chapter Five

The next morning, I got up a half hour earlier than usual to fix my hair and apply makeup the way Betty had taught me. Then I put on the new clothes I'd bought yesterday with my birthday money and stood in front of the full-length mirror on the back of my bedroom door.

I couldn't believe the difference the makeover had made. I looked like a new person—a more vibrant, alive person. The rose outfit emphasized the pink color in my cheeks. It's amazing how different you can look when you're excited.

I couldn't wait to see Mom and Dad's reaction to the new me. Last night, I'd run up to my room when I got home and called "Good night" through the bedroom door when I heard my parents go up to bed. So they were in for a surprise.

By the time I was dressed and ready, Mom and Dad were already in the kitchen having breakfast. Joe had early swim practice, so he'd already left for school.

I sneaked downstairs very quietly so they wouldn't hear me coming, tiptoed to the swinging kitchen door, then burst into the room. "Ta da!" I called out, making a grand entrance.

My dad was sitting at the kitchen table, smoking his pipe. When he glanced up at me, his pipe slid out of his mouth and clattered noisily on the tabletop. He sat up straight and stared at me. *"Claire?"* he asked.

Mom turned around from the kitchen sink, and her mouth dropped open.

"Claire!" she said, and then she started to smile. "You look—fantastic!" Now she was grinning from ear to ear. "What a change!"

Good old Mom always comes through.

"Like it?" I asked Dad, grinning.

He leaned forward and stared at me hard. "Which part?" he asked. "The hair, the face or the clothes?"

"Everything!" I said. "What's the verdict?"

"You really look different," he mumbled.

"Yes, I know, but do you like it?" I asked.

I turned around so he could see the new me from all angles. He still had that look of astonishment on his face.

"Doesn't she look adorable, Tom?" Mom

said, crossing to Dad and nudging his shoulder with her hand. "Just look at your daughter! Isn't she beautiful?"

My dad picked up his pipe. "Just don't let her out of the house," he said.

"What!" I cried. "Are you kidding? Don't you think I look great?"

"Of course he's kidding," Mom assured me. "Aren't you, Tom? Tell your daughter you're kidding."

"I'm kidding," he said. "You look nice."

"Come on, Dad," I said, determined to tease him a little. "Just 'nice'? How about lovely, gorgeous, stunning, good-enough-to-chew-on—"

"What was that last one?" he asked.

"I heard that on a soap opera," I said.

"Oh," he said. "I think I'll stick to my first adjective. You look nice."

I sighed. "Thanks, Dad." I guess I had to be grateful for small favors.

When I got to school, I was ecstatic about everyone's reaction to me. I heard a lot of comments whispered as I walked down the hall, almost as many as the day I'd gotten the Golden Girl job.

"Wow! Look at her!"

"Talk about a glamorous job!"

"What a difference! Is that really Claire?"

"She looks beautiful!"

I can't tell you how *good* I felt! Yesterday I'd

thought that everyone was whispering that I wasn't pretty enough to be the Golden Girl, but today I was sure they agreed that Mr. Trent had made the best possible choice.

Audrey was waiting for me at my locker as usual, and she saw me coming from a long way off. She'd been leaning against my locker, holding her books to her chest. When she saw me, she took a step away from the locker, stood up straight, and lowered her arms. Her mouth was hanging open wide enough for insects to fly in.

I smiled and waved at my best friend.

"Claire Montgomery, what have you *done* to yourself?" she asked.

My smile faded and I stopped about five feet from her. "What do you mean?" I asked. "Don't you like the new me?"

She stared at me for at least thirty seconds before answering. Then she said something so softly that I couldn't hear her.

"What did you say?" I asked. I wasn't sure what was going on. Audrey had never looked so strange.

She looked at the floor a moment, then looked back up at me. "I said, 'I liked the old Claire. She was my best friend.' "

"But I'm *still* your best friend!" I said. "I haven't changed, not on the inside. Just the outside is different. Really, Audrey."

"Okay. We'll see," she said simply.

"What do you mean by that?" I asked, beginning to feel a little annoyed. Your best friend is supposed to be happy for you when something nice happens—at least that's what I've always thought.

"Nothing," she said. "I know you're my friend." She glanced up at the clock on the wall above our heads. "I have to get to my first class. See you later."

She turned and walked down the hall away from me.

"Audrey?" I called out. She stopped and turned back toward me. "Your first class is American lit. You're going the wrong way."

She stared at me a moment, then sighed deeply. As she walked by, she mumbled, "You look fantastic, and I'm going to kill myself." I was too stunned to answer. She stopped a few feet beyond me and turned back. "I was kidding. About killing myself, I mean. You really do look fantastic. I was just worried that . . . well, with your new job and everything, you'd forget all about me. But I really *am* happy for you."

"Thanks, Audrey," I said quietly. "Your opinion means a lot to me."

"Really?"

I shrugged. "Maybe not as much as Ben Riley's, but it means a lot." Then I laughed. "Just kidding."

She grinned. "Thanks. Will you show me how to do my eyes like that?"

"You bet," I answered, feeling relieved.

For the first time in my life I felt very popular and accepted. Everybody congratulated my new and improved looks during the day—except Lana Boyson, of course. I was standing in the hall with some girls from my math class just before third period when she walked by. She did a double take and her friend nudged her in the ribs and grinned.

"What'd I tell you?" Lana's friend said, loud enough for me to hear. "Makeup today, plastic surgery tomorrow."

Lana apparently thought this was a very witty comment, because she laughed uproariously. "I guess miracles do happen!" Their cruel laughter followed me all the way down the hall.

"She's so jealous, she can hardly stand it," said one of my classmates.

"She's so jealous, *I* can hardly stand it," I said ruefully, and the girls around me laughed. "And for that matter, what does she have to be jealous about?"

"She's jealous," one girl said, "because for the first time in her life, she *didn't* win a contest that depended on her looks. She's always gotten everything she wanted. She can't take losing."

After math class, I was walking down the hall and sensed that someone was directly behind me. I turned and looked into the face of Jake Duncan, a senior, very popular with the girls, and the quarterback of our state-champion football team.

He grinned. "Hi, I'm Jake," he said.

"Hi, I'm Stunned," I said.

" 'Stunned'?"

"That you'd think I wouldn't know who you are!" I said. His grin widened. "I cheer you on to victory along with the rest of Lincoln High during every home football game."

"So that's why we're on a winning streak!" he said.

Jake had rugged good looks, like a tough street kid in a movie like *The Outsiders*. Right now, though, he was being very charming. I wished Ben Riley could see me now. Why was I even *thinking* about Ben when I was talking to someone a whole lot more exciting?

"Congratulations," he said. "You must've had a lot of competition for the Golden Girl job."

I wasn't sure how to answer that. There *was* a lot of competition, but it seemed rather ungracious of me to say, "Well, yeah, as a matter of fact, I did beat out two hundred girls."

So I shrugged and said, "Oh, I don't know."

"You're too modest," he said. "I know a lot

of girls who tried out for the job. You obviously impressed the people at Trent's."

I didn't know how to answer that one either, and I was starting to get flustered. I batted my eyelashes in an exaggerated flutter, grinned, and said in my best—though it came out like my worst—Southern belle accent. "You do say the *nah-cest* thangs."

He was obviously surprised by my reaction, because he took a step back.

I tried to make up for my blunder by becoming more serious. "Have you decided on what you're going to do after high school? Have you been offered any football scholarships?" I blurted out.

Good grief! Even talking about the weather would've been more subtle! Now he knows I didn't know what to say.

"Uh, yeah, a few," he said, loping along beside me. Then he stopped in front of a classroom door. "Well, here's my English class. I guess I'll see you."

"Right," I said, wanting to die. "See you later."

You blew it! You blew it! He thinks you're an idiot—and with good reason!

Becoming the Golden Girl had really turned my world upside-down in a hurry. My best friend was acting weird, I suddenly had lots of new friends who didn't notice me before, and I was acting like a nincompoop with the most popular guy in school. All the attention was coming so fast, I didn't know how to handle it.

So when I saw Ben walking toward me after school, I steeled myself for the worst to happen. He approached with a smile.

"You're making quite a hit today," he said. "Everyone's talking about you all over school."

"Oh, yeah," I said quietly. "It's been a very—unusual day."

He grinned. "I feel a little like Henry Higgins in *My Fair Lady*."

I sighed, thinking about what Audrey had said. "Just call me Eliza," I said quite seriously, in a Cockney accent that was a vast improvement over my Southern belle.

"Hey, you do that accent pretty well," Ben said.

"Thanks," I said, forcing a smile and wishing that Ben weren't so darned cute. As he stood there smiling, I looked into his eyes and *ached* because I liked him so much. But I tried to remain cool. "What's new?"

"Dad said to tell you that you'll be the commentator at Trent's spring fashion show. You know, the MC." He smiled. "He said the news would probably make your day. It's the biggest event of the season."

"What?" I said, taking a step back. "The MC? Me? Are you sure?"

"Sure I'm sure," he said, grinning. "Isn't that great?"

My throat constricted all of a sudden, and I tried to swallow, but I couldn't. "But I—I—I can't do it!" I stammered. "I mean, I can't stand there in front of all those people!"

Ben looked confused. "What do you mean, you can't do it? It's part of your duties as the Golden Girl."

I took another step back. "But the Golden Girl has never had to be an MC before!" I said.

"This is the first year. Mr. Trent wants to showcase the store's spokesperson—that's you—at the fashion show. He wants to make it an annual tradition. He thinks you'll be good. And you *will* be!"

"No, I won't!" I cried. "Because I won't *be* there!"

Ben's face fell then and it made me feel terrible, because I knew that I was letting him down, but I couldn't help it. I *couldn't* be the MC at the fashion show!

"That's part of your job, Claire," he said, obviously irritated. "When you auditioned to be the Golden Girl, you should have done so with the understanding that if you were chosen, you would represent Trent's Department Store whenever you were called upon to do so."

"But, Ben, there will be *hundreds* of people at that fashion show! Oh, just the thought of it is making me dizzy!" I gasped.

"So what's the problem?" Ben looked as if he didn't know whether to sit me down and give me a glass of water or punch me in the nose.

"So . . ." I paused. "So—I get stage fright, that's what."

Ben stared at me a minute. "Stage fright? How did you manage to audition so well?"

"That's different!" I said. "It was just you and me in the studio. A few people don't bother me. But I can't stand up in front of a *crowd*!"

Ben stared at me a moment. "You get stage fright in front of a crowd, but not a camera?"

"That's right," I said. "I know it must sound silly to you, but I don't know how to explain it any other way."

Ben reached out and took my hand. His hand felt warm and comforting, and I was glad that he wanted to reassure me. But there was nothing even Ben Riley could do to make me feel better about performing in front of all those people.

"Claire, lots of people get stage fright, even famous people who make their living performing."

"I know," I said, feeling defensive.

"You know who Carly Simon is? And Johnny Mathis?"

"The singers? Of course."

"They get stage fright every time they perform," Ben said. "I've read interviews with both of them, and they talked about how frightened they are to be in front of people."

"Really? Carly Simon? I really like her. Mom says she was always her favorite singer."

"But they go out and do what they're hired to do—they sing and make millions of people happy."

"Well, I hardly think that my presence at the Trent fashion show is going to make millions of people happy," I said.

"No, but it'll make Mr. Trent happy, and he's the guy we've got to please." Ben squeezed my hand, reached up, and brushed away a stray strand of hair from my face.

I sighed deeply. How could I turn Ben down? He was counting on me. "Well, I'll *try*, Ben, but I can't promise you anything . . . that I'll show up, for instance."

Ben grinned. "Of course you'll show up," he said, "if I have to come over to your house and drag you there myself."

"When is this wonderful event taking place?" I asked.

"Next month," he said.

"For spring? In February?"

"Sure. Trent's begins to get their spring clothes in after inventory in early January," Ben explained.

"Oh. I just don't know, Ben."

"You'll be great," Ben said.

"What if I get the hiccups?" I asked. "You wouldn't think I was so great if I got a bad case of hiccups right in the middle of the show."

Ben smiled. "Why do you think you'd get the hiccups on that particular night?" he asked.

"Because, I have a history of getting the hiccups when I'm nervous about being in front of a crowd."

"But what about the time you played Ophelia?" he asked. "That went well, didn't it?"

"Not exactly," I admitted. "Ophelia had a very bad case of the hiccups." Ben didn't say anything. "But don't worry. No one will be able to hear my hiccups anyway, because of the racket my knees will make when they knock together."

"We'll amplify your voice. You'll have a microphone."

I stared at him. "Have you ever heard hiccups amplified over a public-address system?" I groaned and covered my face with my hands.

Ben laughed and gently pried my hands away from my face. "You *won't* get the hiccups! I have a foolproof method of stopping them."

"What's your method?"

"Never mind. It helps to have the element of surprise."

"I just don't know."

"Don't keep saying that. Plan on being the MC in February," he said. "And I'll see you tomorrow night at KIRQ, all right? Oh, I nearly forgot." He pulled a piece of paper out of his pocket. "Here's the copy for the TV spot. There'll be a TelePrompTer, so you don't need to memorize it, but make sure you're familiar with it."

"I'm looking forward to the TV spot, at least," I said, unfolding the paper.

"Good," he said, gazing into my eyes. "So am I." He gave my arm a squeeze.

I watched Ben as he disappeared down the hall. I wanted to be the MC in the fashion show to please him, but the thought of actually doing it terrified me.

I laughed to myself. Boy, I knew I must be pretty hung up on Ben if I'd even *consider* the MC job. There was no one else in the world who could convince me to try something like that. Not even Jake Duncan.

I leaned against the lockers behind me. Jake was really cool, a football hero and very popular, but when I talked to him, I didn't feel the way I did when I talked to Ben. With Ben, I felt a warm, comfortable feeling inside. I could be myself with Ben. We could joke around and even act a little goofy. But Jake was different. I would always be on my guard with Jake, and I knew our conversation had been really stiff.

I liked the way Ben was so understanding about my stage fright. I just hoped that he would be as understanding on the night of the fashion show as he was today!

Chapter Six

On Friday night, I arrived at the TV station thirty minutes early to dress and put on my makeup—Ben had told me there was a lighted mirror in the rest room. While I was doing my face, I tried to calm myself down.

I stood in front of the big mirror and inspected myself from various angles to see if I looked okay. I nervously gave myself a pep talk to build up my self-confidence.

"You're *gorgeous*. You're sophistication personified. You are the kind of woman that men want to *die* for."

I stopped then and stared at myself in the mirror, sticking out my tongue at my reflection. Then I flounced out of the rest room in my flimsy, sexy dress and heels.

"Hey, you look fantastic," Ben said when he saw me. "Doesn't she, Alec?" he asked the bearded man standing next to him in the hall outside of the rest room.

"Good enough to chew on," Alec said, grinning.

Alec must've watched the same soap opera I did.

"Alec is the engineer tonight," Ben said. "He'll be working with us on most of the Trent spots."

"Hi, Alec," I said. "Thanks for the compliment."

Then I realized that it was the first compliment I'd received without blushing or getting tongue-tied. It wasn't hard to accept the compliment, either. All I had to do was simply say, "Thank you." I guess accepting compliments gets easier with practice.

"Let's go down to the studio," Ben said to me. "Alec, we'll see you later."

Alec left, and Ben and I walked to the studio down the hall. Ben pulled open the double doors and we walked inside.

The studio wasn't as dark as it had been at the audition. Two men dressed in dark suits were chatting with their hands in their pockets. Ben led me over to them.

"Well, this must be Claire Montgomery, our new Golden Girl." One of the men extended his hand to me and smiled. "I'm Pete Riley, Ben's father." He looked really distinguished—

tall, with graying hair at the temples, and Ben's clear blue eyes.

I shook his hand. "And this," he said, gesturing to the other man, "is Mr. Trent, owner of Trent's Department Store."

Mr. Trent was also handsome, but older, with a head of thick, white hair and steely gray eyes.

"Hello, I'm glad to meet you," I said as I shook Mr. Trent's hand.

Mr. Trent nodded crisply and said, "Hello, young lady. Are you ready to go to work?"

"Yes, I am," I said.

"Splendid, splendid." Mr. Trent stood with his arms behind him, rocking very slightly back and forth. "And I'm looking forward to having you MC our fashion show this year. You'll be the first Golden Girl ever to have that honor." He studied my face for my reaction.

I felt the smile on my face fading and I glanced at Ben. He frowned meaningfully and nodded.

I forced a smile. "Th-thank you, Mr. Trent," I stammered, my palms beginning to sweat. "I'll do my best."

"I'm sure you will," he said. He looked at Mr. Riley. "Ready to get to work? Studio time is expensive."

Mr. Riley and Mr. Trent left to go up to the production booth.

"Ready?" Ben asked me. "Did you practice your lines?"

"Yes," I said. "I'm ready."

I'd practiced my lines in front of the mirror a lot at home. First, I tried delivering them in a very sexy voice; then I did them in a bubbly-cheerleader voice, sort of hopping from foot to foot and giggling; then, to top it off, I sang the commercial like an opera singer, with big, grand gestures. These mirror performances would have looked pretty strange if someone had watched me, but I think they loosened me up a little, and I certainly became familiar with the lines.

"Great," Ben said. The blue screen was hanging down on the floor as it had been during the auditions, and Ben gestured to it. "Go and stand over there, Claire," he said. The camera was already pointing at that spot.

"Can you hear me, Claire?" Mr. Riley's voice boomed over the sound system .

"Loud and clear," I said.

"Good. We really liked your audition, so for this commercial, we'd like to have you give us a similar reading. Try to give us the same tone and enthusiasm, and the same bright expression."

"Okay, sure," I said, feeling suddenly confident. I felt as if I needed to warm up a little, though, so I looked into the camera and planted a huge, clown-like smile on my face. "This is my lucky day!" I called out happily.

"What was that, Claire?" Mr. Riley asked over the intercom.

"Oh," I said, startled. "Sorry, I was just warming up. I didn't know you were listening —uh, I didn't know you could hear me."

"That's not the kind of smile we want from her, Pete," Mr. Trent said.

"No, I think she's just warming up," Mr. Riley answered.

Ben winked at me and whispered, "They can see and hear everything from up there."

"Well, in that case, don't blow any kisses at me," I joked.

Ben grinned. "Aw, shucks. That was my next move."

I laughed.

"Can we get a voice reading, Claire?" Mr. Riley interrupted.

"A what?"

"Just talk to me a minute so Alec can set the levels."

"Uh, sure," I said, suddenly tongue-tied. *What should I say?* "Hi, folks," I said, looking directly into the camera. "My name is Whitney Houston and I'd like to sing a song for you." Ben's face appeared around the side of the camera. He rolled his eyes, smiled, and shook his head. I looked up at the production booth. "Is that enough?"

"I don't know about you guys, but I want to hear the song," Alec said teasingly.

"Let's move along," Mr. Trent said, sounding a little nervous. "Studio time is expensive."

"That will do, Claire," Ben's father said. "Now let's have you read the copy into the camera."

"Okay." I gazed into the lens and read from the TelePrompTer.

"Hi, I'm Claire, Trent's new Golden Girl. Trent's has some exciting plans for this year, and I can't wait to tell you about them. The first event is the annual Golden Girl sale. Everything in the store will be drastically reduced from January 26 to 28. I'll be there to say hi, so stop in at Trent's and see me while you shop for terrific bargains. Remember, January 26 to 28. Come on out. I'll be looking for you!"

When I finished reading, Ben leaned around the camera and gave me the A-OK signal with his thumb and index finger. Then he spoke into his headset. "Did we pick the right girl, or what!"

"We sure did!" Mr. Riley said over the sound system. "That was a very good reading, Claire. I can tell you practiced your lines."

"Thank you," I said, thrilled that my mirror practice had paid off.

Mr. Trent spoke up. "I'd like to see her use some gestures during the commercial. For instance, when she says, 'Hi, I'm Claire,' she could wave into the camera. And then when she says, 'I'll be there' and 'while you shop,' she could point to herself and then into the camera, at the audience."

Those sounded like very corny, contrived gestures to me, and I glanced at Ben. He was listening with a worried frown on his face. He looked up at me and rolled his eyes, but pressed a finger to his lips.

The intercom clicked off. I figured Mr. Riley was discussing Mr. Trent's ridiculous suggestions with him.

After a minute or two, the intercom clicked back on. "Okay, Claire," Mr. Riley said. "We're going to try Mr. Trent's suggestions. Did you hear them?"

"Uh, yes," I said.

Ben looked at the floor and shook his head.

This is going to be awful, I thought. *I can't believe the owner of the store is going to ruin his own commercial!*

"Okay, then, Claire," Ben's father said, sounding rather tired. "Let's try it again."

The red light came on in the front of the camera, and I began. I intentionally exaggerated the wave and gave a bigger than necessary grin, hoping that Mr. Trent would see how ridiculous it looked. And when I pointed into the camera, I pushed my hand up almost into the lense so that it blocked out the rest of me in the picture.

When I'd finished, I glanced up at Ben. He obviously realized why I had overdone the gestures, and was grinning from ear to ear and nodding his approval.

I grinned back.

After a moment, Mr. Riley came on over the intercom. "Claire," he said, "let's drop the gestures. Just give us lots of genuine enthusiasm."

Ben winked at me. Obviously my overdone performance had worked.

"Okay," I called out. "I'm ready."

The red light winked on again and I started reading the lines. I was looking into the camera lense, but I was aware that Ben was not looking through the camera. His face was just to the side of the camera, and in my peripheral vision, I could see that he had his thumbs stuck in his ears and was wiggling the rest of his fingers and making faces at me!

I was so surprised that I sputtered and doubled over in laughter.

The intercom clicked on. "What happened there, Claire?" Mr. Riley asked. "It was going really well until you started laughing. Is something wrong?"

I got control of myself and stood up straight again. I looked into the camera. "I'm sorry," I said. "I'm ready to try it again."

I stepped out of camera range, made a face at Ben, then stepped back into the camera spot.

"Okay," I said, "I'm ready."

This time Ben remained behind the camera and I gave my best reading ever.

When I was finished, the intercom clicked on. "Great!" Mr. Riley shouted over the speaker. "Let's play it back. Claire, watch the monitor in the studio."

It was the first time I'd ever seen myself on TV and I closed my eyes through most of it. I thought I looked like a chipmunk—the camera was focused so closely on me.

"Help," I groaned, but Ben gently removed my hands from my face.

"You're sensational!" Ben whispered when it was over.

"Terrific, Claire!" Mr. Riley announced over the speaker. "That's a take. You're a real pro. Excellent job."

Ben turned to me, grinning. "They love you," he said.

I was so ecstatic that I spoke without thinking. "And what about you?" I said.

"What—?" He looked at me quizzically.

Then I realized how bold I'd sounded. "Oh, that came out all wrong," I said, laughing nervously. "I, uh, just wondered if you liked my reading." I made a joke to cover my embarrassment. "Didn't you love my delivery? Did I move you to tears or change your life in any significant way?"

Ben laughed. "You're really something, Claire," he said, "I've never met a girl like you."

"Care to be specific?" I asked, feeling playful.

Ben gazed at me intensely, as if to focus on the inside part of me behind my eyes.

"You're intelligent, funny, and just a little bit nuts." He grinned and touched the tip of my nose with his finger. "And somewhat cute."

"Oh, rats, I was hoping you'd say ravishingly beautiful."

His smile widened. "That's what I mean. Just a little bit nuts."

I imitated the face he'd made at me earlier by putting my thumbs in my ears and sticking out my tongue. "Look who's talking," I said.

Ben laughed, put his arm around my shoulders, and gave me a squeeze.

"Ben?" Mr. Riley's voice boomed over the sound system.

"Yes, Dad?" he said.

"We're ready," Mr. Riley said. "You want to come up and watch the mixing?"

"Absolutely. Be right up." Ben turned back to me. "Want to come up and see how it's done?"

"What are you mixing?" I asked.

"We're going to add the Trent jingle to your video and add some Chyrons."

"What's a—"

"Come on. I'll show you."

Ben grabbed my hand and we hurried out of the studio and up to the production room.

Mr. Trent, Mr. Riley, and Alec sat behind a large production panel filled with dials, levers, and lights. All three were smiling when Ben and I walked in.

Mr. Trent reached over and shook my hand. "Very nicely done, Ms. Montgomery," he said.

Ben, now standing just behind Mr. Trent, winked at me. "Thank you," I said. I can't describe how it felt when Ben winked at me. All I know is that it felt better than anything else in the world.

Mr. Riley rolled up a couple of chairs on wheels for us and we sat down.

Alec was playing back the video of the commercial on one of the screens over the production panel.

"First, we need to see Trent's," Mr. Riley said, and Alec punched a button that caused a picture of the store to appear on the screen. "At the same time, we should hear the Trent's jingle."

Alec threaded an audiotape through a machine in front of him, and played it so we could hear.

Ben leaned over. "See?" he whispered, his eyes sparkling mischievously. "You aren't the star you thought you were. Trent's Department Store is the real star here."

"Yes," I whispered back, "but you couldn't have done it without me."

Ben grinned. "Right."

Alec fast-forwarded the tape of my commercial to find a particular spot. My voice sounded like a chipmunk chattering away in an unintelligible garble, while my face appeared to be a whir of funny facial expressions.

"Gee, isn't it great how videotape can really capture a person's essence!" Ben quipped.

I playfully whacked him on the arm. The adults in the room were too busy to notice.

I learned that a Chyron is a line of letters thrown up on the screen in front of the picture. Mr. Riley had Alec use the store's name and the dates of the Golden Girl sale in Chyrons.

The commercial was mixed and ready to go in about forty-five minutes. Mr. Trent, Mr. Riley, and Alec got up and strolled into the hall, putting on their coats as they discussed the basketball game they'd all seen on TV the night before.

Ben and I sat alone in the production booth.

"You were pretty good, Claire," Ben said, leaning back in his chair, his hands behind his head. "I especially liked the chipmunk imitation."

I grinned. "I know. A performance that fast takes incredible talent and lots of hard work." I paused. "But you know what they say about all work and no play . . ."

"Your social life is important to you, I take it?" Ben said, with mock seriousness.

"The most important part of all," I said, playing along.

There was a pause as Ben dropped the game. He gazed into my eyes and smiled. "Well, since we agree about how important it is, how would you feel about—"

"Ben?" Mr. Riley poked his head in the door.

What lousy timing! I wanted to throw something at him.

"We're ready to go," Mr. Riley said. "Claire, do you need a ride home?"

"Uh, no thank you," I said. "My dad is coming to pick me up. Thanks anyway."

Mr. Riley nodded and ducked out the door.

I looked into Ben's eyes. "You were saying?" I said, but the spell was definitely broken.

Ben smiled. "We'll have to finish up where we left off sometime."

"Any particular time?" I hinted.

"Soon," he said. He squeezed my hand. "See

you later, Claire. You were great today. But you have to promise me one thing."

"What's that?" I asked curiously.

"That you'll remember me when you're a movie star."

I swatted Ben playfully as he left the room—I was in the mood for romance, not for jokes! But I guess it couldn't hurt to have a boy-friend with a good sense of humor.

Boy, was I getting ahead of myself!

Chapter Seven

"I love our games against North High," Audrey said as we filed into the school gym. "Especially when we demolish them. Think we'll kill 'em tonight, Claire?"

"I hope so," I said. "We're favored by eight points."

I let my eyes sweep over the crowd, searching for Ben Riley's face. I knew that he wore a navy-blue coat, so my gaze automatically paused every time I saw that color.

The basketball games against North High are among the most popular events at school, and tonight was our last shot at the state championship.

Audrey and I pressed through the crowd and found seats about halfway up in the middle section of bleachers. Before I sat down, I scanned the crowd one more time, alert for

Ben's thick, dark hair. I didn't see Ben, but one other face caught my eye.

Lana Boyson. She had seen me, too, and was making her way toward us, with two of the girls from her clique trailing behind her.

Oh, no, I thought, *this is not a good way to start the evening.* "Looking for Ben?" Audrey shouted over the noise of the Lincoln pep band.

"Shh! Don't look now, but Lana Boyson saw us and is heading this way. I'm afraid she's going to sit near us."

"Where? I don't see Lana Boyson—oh." Audrey turned around just as Lana sat down right beside her.

"Well, here we are, sitting right next to the Golden Girl and her entourage. I feel so honored," Lana sneered. "Don't you feel honored, girls?"

The two girls at her side nodded. "Honored," they said like puppets.

"Why is it that we are so fortunate?" Lana continued sarcastically.

Audrey turned around and smiled sweetly. "Just lucky, I guess."

I shoved my elbow into Audrey's ribs to quiet her, and she stifled a giggle. A couple of girls sitting in front of us had heard our conversation, and they turned around and laughed, which got Audrey giggling again.

Lana was obviously angry. She scowled at

me. "Think you're pretty hot stuff now, don't you, Golden Girl?" Lana said. "Boys who normally wouldn't give you the time of day are now giving you a lot of attention. Isn't it great to be popular? I've always enjoyed it myself."

I didn't answer or even turn around. I just wished she'd disappear. "And you got yourself a makeover. You don't even look like the same person. But then again, you really did need some help in that department."

"Oh, shut up, Lana. Claire looks great," said one of Joe's friends who was sitting nearby.

"Okay," I said, finally turning around. "That's enough."

I could feel the eyes of about a dozen kids on us. Unfortunately, our squabble was attracting more attention than the game.

Lana's face turned bright red as soon as I spoke, and she stood up abruptly. "You'd better watch your step, Golden Girl—"

"The name is Claire," I said calmly.

"Whatever. You're just a Plain Jane who got lucky, that's all. Ben Riley—or any other person, for that matter—will see you for what you are when you're finished being the Golden Girl."

And with that, she turned and began to push her way down the bleacher steps.

The crowd around us laughed and cheered.

A few of them even clapped. Apparently, Lana wasn't as popular as she thought she was.

I was glad that I'd won the battle, but I wondered if there was any truth to Lana's words. What if she was right?

At halftime, we were ahead, 42–38. I usually like to stay in the stands during halftime to see the show presented by the cheerleaders and pep band or the school jazz ensemble. But tonight, I was thinking a lot about Ben, and I hoped I'd bump into him if I wandered out into the hall.

"I'm really thirsty," I said to Audrey. "Let's go get a soda."

"And besides, Ben might be out there," she said.

I laughed. "You know me too well."

Slowly, with crowds of people milling around us, we made our way into the hall. We waited in line for several minutes before we could buy our colas, then moved to a less crowded area of the foyer near the outside doors.

Suddenly I remembered something. "Do you think the rest of the school is open?" I asked Audrey.

"I don't know," she said. "Why?"

I rolled my eyes and sighed heavily. "I've got a math test on Monday and I forgot my book. I need to get to my locker."

"Go ahead and try," Audrey said. "I'll hold your drink for you."

"Thanks." I handed her my cup and hurried down the dark hallway. I'd never traveled inside the school without the lights on, and although I knew my way, it was still kind of spooky.

I reached my locker—it was the second from the end, so it was very easy to find—opened it, and grabbed my book.

I was about halfway back to the gym when a figure stepped out of the shadows and blocked my way.

"So you're the famous Golden Girl," the girl said. Her voice was cold. "You don't look so special to me."

All I could see was her silhouette. Her face was partially hidden in the darkness, with the lights from the gym at her back.

I joked to hide my nervousness. "That's because you don't know me."

The girl was silent. I edged closer to her and saw that she was tall and blond, with short, curly hair. The girl was wearing a long raccoon coat and leather boots. She was so sophisticated-looking that I just stood there staring at her.

"Do you know who I am?" she asked, looming above me in her high-heeled boots.

"No, I guess not," I said. "Should I?"

"I'm Jennifer Perkins." She seemed to think that I'd recognize the name.

"Okay, Jennifer Perkins," I said, still not

101

sure what was going on. "Now we've met. What do you want?"

She made an impatient little noise and shifted her weight to her other hip. "I'm Ben Riley's girlfriend."

My mouth dropped open before I could stop it.

"You'd better watch yourself," she said. "Ben is off-limits to you, understand?"

"Jennifer?" It was Ben's voice. "Are you down here?" Ben emerged from around the corner. He approached us holding two large cups. When he was close enough to see me, he stopped short.

"Hi, Claire," he said softly.

"Hi," I said.

There was an awkward pause as he glanced from Jennifer to me and back to Jennifer again. "Uh, did you two meet each other? Jen, this is Claire Montgomery, Claire, this—"

"We've met," Jennifer said coldly, glaring at me over her fur collar. "I was just telling her that North is going to cream Lincoln tonight."

Ben laughed uncomfortably. "Don't be too sure of that. Lincoln's ahead and playing well."

"Come on, Ben," Jennifer said then, her tone becoming coy. "Let's go. I'm dying of thirst."

She took one of Ben's arms and led him down the hall to the gym. He threw me a quick smile over his shoulder before he disappeared into the crowd.

I stood in the darkness for a moment to collect myself, then slowly made my way back to the gym.

"Boy, that sure took a long time," Audrey said, still holding my soda. "Halftime is almost over."

I told Audrey what had happened with Jennifer and Ben.

"Nice girl," Audrey commented. "What's her problem, anyway?"

"I don't know," I said flippantly. "And I don't care."

I tasted my cola. It was watery, so I dumped it down the drain of the drinking fountain nearby and tossed the cup in the waste can. Then I leaned against the wall and groaned. "I'm *so* stupid!"

"Oh, yeah?" Audrey asked. "How come?"

"Because I *do* care!" I said. "I care about that guy Ben Riley. I care that he has a girlfriend, and that he's at this game with Jennifer Perkins and not me!"

Audrey patted my arm. "I know," she said. "But just think about it for a minute. If he has such bad taste, why would you want to be with him anyway? Besides, if you were with him, you wouldn't get to be with me right now."

I laughed. "Audrey, you're the best. You're my favorite date any day."

Suddenly I looked up and saw Lana Boyson leaning against a wall, watching Audrey and me. She sauntered over to us, a malicious smile on her face.

"What's the matter, Claire?" she asked. "He never was your boyfriend and he never will be. Even if he breaks up with Jennifer, he'd never be interested in you."

"And I suppose you're assuming he'd prefer you, Lana," Audrey burst out angrily.

I was very quickly getting a monstrous migraine.

"I *know* he would," Lana said.

"Come on," Audrey laughed. "The guy's got some class—"

"This is unreal," I said, clutching my throbbing head with both hands. "I can't believe you're saying this stuff to me, Lana. I thought people only talked like this on soap operas."

Lana stalked off with a haughty toss of her head.

"You okay?" Audrey asked me.

"I've never had such a pounding headache," I answered.

"Want to go home?" Audrey asked.

"Yeah," I said. "I've had enough for one night, that's for sure. Wait here, and I'll go and call my dad for a ride."

I fished some change out of my pocket and

dialed home. I let it ring eight times before I gave up.

"They're not home," I told Audrey, who was waiting by the exit doors. "I guess we'll have to walk."

The trip wasn't long—less than a mile—but the temperature was in the 20s. There was a brisk wind, and we thought we'd freeze to death for sure before arriving home.

Finally we got to my front door. Audrey and I stomped the snow off our boots, then hurried inside.

"Want some cocoa?" I asked.

"I was hoping you'd ask!" Audrey said, rubbing her cold, red hands together. "Can I turn on the TV? Maybe there's a good movie on."

"Sure," I said.

Audrey trudged into the family room, still wearing her bulky down coat. Just then the front door opened, and Mom, Dad, and Joe piled into the living room.

"Hi, guys," I said. "Where were you?"

"We went out to dinner," Mom said. "What happened to the basketball game?"

Just then a high-pitched squeal sounded from the family room. "Claire! Come quick! You're on TV!"

All of us ran into the family room. Audrey was jumping up and down, she was so excited.

It was really weird to stand in my own house and see myself on TV. I'd seen the commercial at the studio just after we taped it, but it was different seeing myself on the same TV where I'd seen *Gone With the Wind* and *Roots.*

It was over in a flash, unfortunately. Audrey clapped me on the back and Joe picked me up and swung me around. Mom hugged me and exclaimed that it was the best local TV commercial she'd ever seen. Even Dad yelled "Terrific!" and put his arm around my shoulders.

I was really proud of it. I think I did a pretty good job, and the spot looked very classy.

"I wonder what Lana will say when she sees it," Audrey whispered. "She's going to be positively *green!*"

I shivered. "I don't want to think about Lana," I said. "Tonight I just want to enjoy being a star!"

Chapter Eight

"I saw you on TV!"

That was the first thing I heard when I walked into school on Monday. I wasn't sure how to respond to the girl in my science class, so I just smiled and said, "Oh, yes, I caught it, too."

"Hey, you were great in the Trent's commercial!" another girl I didn't know called out as I was walking down the hall.

"Hiya, beautiful!" one of Joe's friends said, grinning, as he passed me in the hall. "You were great on TV last night. I saw it twice!" That was a surprise to me. I didn't know they'd run the spot more than once. I was feeling pretty good as I walked to homeroom.

But the minute I rounded the corner into the room, I knew something was up. Audrey was sitting at her desk, closest to the door. Her face was red and she looked very angry. A couple of the kids were laughing as they watched what was going on at the front of the room.

I stopped just inside the door and my mouth dropped open.

Lana Boyson was standing behind the podium at the front of the classroom. She had obviously made herself up to look like me. She'd teased her hair into a style similar to mine, and was wearing tons of makeup. She smiled out at the class in an exaggerated imitation of me. "So come on out to the Golden Girl sale! I'll be looking for you!" she announced, batting her eyelashes.

When the kids saw me standing there, the room fell silent. Lana stopped and turned toward me, then flashed me an exaggerated smile. "Hi, Claire!"

The tightness in my chest returned as my heart hammered wildly. My face was hot and I could feel the tears coming. But I wasn't going to give Lana the satisfaction of seeing me cry. I turned and ran out of the room, down the hall, to the bathroom. I closed myself up in one of the stalls.

After a few minutes, the bathroom door opened and I could hear someone come in.

"Claire?" It was Audrey. "She was just awful, and I got so mad. I'm sorry you had to see that. You know she's just jealous. She's so incredibly unhappy and jealous of you that she made a fool out of herself like that in front of a whole class of kids."

I wanted to answer Audrey, but I couldn't stop crying.

"Most of the kids hated what she did. After you ran out, they yelled at her to shut up and stop."

I opened the stall door. "Really?" I said.

Audrey came over and hugged me. "Really. Come on. Let's go back to homeroom. Mrs. Callahan won't know where you are. She was late getting to class or she'd never have let Lana get away with that."

We walked slowly back to class. The day hadn't started off very well, that was for sure. And it didn't get any better when I took my math test. I'd had such a hard time concentrating on homework for the past week or so that I just wasn't prepared for it. I couldn't figure out most of the problems. I knew when I handed it in to Ms. Corcoran that I'd bombed on it, and there was a huge lump in my throat as I walked out of class. My average is usually about a B+, and grades are important to me. I couldn't remember the last time I'd failed a test.

Just after school, I saw Ben in the hall. He saw me and smiled, and I steadied myself, determined to act very cool. Ever since seeing him and Jennifer at the game, I'd decided that I wouldn't allow myself to feel overwhelmed by him anymore. Ben was off-limits, and he wasn't worth the hassle.

"Hey, Claire," he called. "I've been looking for you all day."

"Oh, yeah?" I said casually. "What's up?"

"Nothing, really," he said. "Did you see our spot last night?"

I noticed the *our* right away.

"Yes, as a matter of fact I did," I said.

"Well?" he asked with a grin. "Didn't you think we did a great job? Didn't it look smooth?"

"It was pretty slick," I said.

"My dad's an excellent director and producer," he said. "He makes good choices."

"Yes," I said airily. "Your dad is a very talented guy."

"And so are you," Ben said, his gaze hanging on to mine.

"Yes, I'm a very talented guy, too," I said, not batting an eye.

Ben laughed. "You know what I mean. You were great." Ben shifted his weight over one hip. "Uh, about that night at the basketball game—" he said.

"What about it?" I asked, shrugging indifferently.

"I don't know what Jennifer said to you before I came over—"

"She was talking about the game," I lied.

Ben gazed into my eyes a moment. "Well,

neither of you seemed very comfortable with the conversation . . ."

"It was no big deal," I lied again. "But anyway, I have to get home now. See you around, Ben."

Ben's mouth fell open, and he took a step back, but he didn't try to make me stay and talk to him.

"Right," he said shortly.

It took all the self-discipline I had to walk away from him. What I wanted to do was whirl around and say, "Make me stay and talk! What did you want to say about Jennifer at the game? That she's horrible and disgusting and you hate her? Talk to me; tell me you love me, not Jennifer," and all kinds of crazy things like that.

Of course, I didn't say any of that stuff. I may be a little bit nuts, but I'm not crazy.

Besides, if Ben wasn't going to be a part of my personal life, I would be okay. Even after the Golden Girl job was over and I wasn't a "celebrity" anymore, I would still feel good about myself and have a little head start on feeling like a together, poised adult.

I walked out of the school building, holding my head high, and started out for home.

Chapter Nine

That night I spent an hour closeted in my room studying geometry. After my disastrous test, I thought I'd better get caught up so I didn't flunk out of school. I was determined not to let Ben or Jennifer or Lana mess up my grade-point average. It was bad enough that I'd failed one test; I wasn't going to risk getting grounded and losing the Golden Girl job by failing any more of them. That certainly wouldn't be very glamorous.

When the phone rang, I was just finishing a complicated proof. I'd gotten the right answer, according to the key in the back of the book, and I felt very proud of myself.

I got up and raced to the phone in my parents' room. "Hello?"

"Hi, Claire," the voice said. It was a guy whose voice I didn't recognize. He sounded friendly, though. "It's Jake Duncan."

I nearly dropped the phone. Jake Duncan! Football quarterback Jake Duncan, the guy I'd acted like a fool with just last week!

"Hi, Jake," I said, trying not to sound too surprised.

"How're you doing?" he asked.

"Just fine," I said, feeling much more confident than I had the last time I'd spoken to him. "It's nice to hear your voice."

"Yeah, well, I heard *you* on TV last night," he said. "You were really good."

"Oh, thanks," I said. "I'm glad you liked it." I smiled to myself, thinking how much easier this conversation was than it would've been several weeks ago.

"There's a party on Friday night," he said. "It's at Jeff Lawson's house. Do you want to go?"

"Um, I'm pretty sure I'm free," I said, pretending to check my social schedule. "Yes, I'd love to go." I pinched myself to make sure I wasn't dreaming. I was glad he couldn't see the idiotic grin that was plastered across my face. "It sounds like fun."

"Great," he said. "I'll pick you up at seven."

"Okay," I said, and told him where I lived.

"Well," he said, "if I don't see you at school before then, I'll see you at seven on Friday."

"Terrific," I said, and hung up.

I paced nervously around my room. "Jake Duncan asked me out. . . ." I said to myself.

To be asked out by Jake was almost as big an accomplishment as getting the Golden Girl job—Jake only dated the most popular girls at school. I was really looking forward to the party, but I also felt sort of nervous.

The party was going to be at Jeff Lawson's house, Jake had said. Jeff was part of the most exclusive "in" crowd in the school. He was a senior, president of the student council, and a starting forward on the basketball team. He was also very wealthy—his father was a noted criminal lawyer—and lived in one of the ritziest homes in town. I hoped I could convince everyone at the party that I fit in.

For the rest of the week, I tried my best to concentrate on my school subjects, but it sure wasn't easy. I wondered what having a date with Jake Duncan would be like. I kept thinking about the party on Friday, and whether or not Ben and Jennifer would be there. I didn't see Lana in the hall, which didn't make me too sad, and I didn't see Ben, either. So I really tried to focus on schoolwork. But on Thursday after geometry, Ms. Corcoran called me to her desk.

"Claire, I'm concerned about you," she said.

"Really?" I asked, dreading what my teacher would say next.

"Yes. I'm afraid you failed your test this week." She handed me my test paper, which was covered with red marks.

"I know," I said. "I knew right away that I'd failed it."

"But the problem isn't just your test, Claire," she said. "Your daily work has been pretty sloppy and you haven't been paying attention in class."

"I know," I said, sighing heavily.

"Is it the Golden Girl job?" she asked. "Are the changes in your life overwhelming you right now?"

I've got to hand it to Ms. Corcoran: She's really tuned in to teenagers, unlike most teachers.

"Yes," I admitted. "I guess I am pretty overwhelmed." I looked her right in the eye, determined to show her that I was still the competent sophomore that she'd thought I was. "But I can handle it. I just need to get back on track."

"I hope you're right," Ms. Corcoran said. "I saw your first Trent commercial and it was quite good, but you must realize that nothing is more important than keeping up with your schoolwork. Especially in math, where we build upon what we've learned—"

"I know," I interrupted.

"If you get too far behind, you just might not be able to catch up," Ms. Corcoran added.

"I studied for an hour last night, Ms. Corcoran," I said. "And I'll keep it up until I'm earning A's again."

"I'm glad to hear that," she said.

Because she accepted my promise so easily, I was determined not to disappoint her. So I studied doubly hard the next few days.

By the time Friday night arrived, I felt better about math, but more nervous about the party.

By seven o'clock I was dressed in my best pair of black jeans, my favorite burgundy sweater, and a pair of loafers.

I'd spent at least an hour on my hair and makeup, and I have to say that I looked pretty good. As I stopped in front of the mirror fluffing my hair one last time, I thought about how much my self-confidence had improved in the last couple of weeks. If I'd been invited by Jake Duncan to a party three weeks ago, I'd have been a basket case by the time he came to pick me up.

Mom and Dad casually strolled into the room at five minutes to seven. I was sure they were waiting to see Jake when he arrived.

"Uh, hi, Mom and Dad," I said.

"Hi, honey," Mom said. They planted themselves on the couch.

"Um, Jake's going to be here soon," I said.

"Oh, really?" Mom asked innocently. "That'll be nice."

"No, what I mean is . . . are you two going to be here?"

"Well, I guess so," Mom said. "I'm going to

start this new book I borrowed from the library." She held up a thick novel.

"Why don't you both go *upstairs* and read?" I suggested.

"Why?" Mom asked.

"Because I'm afraid you're going to ask Jake a lot of questions," I said. "I just want to be alone when he gets here."

"Honey, we wouldn't ask your boyfriend too many questions—"

"He's *not* my boyfriend!" I cried. "We're just going to a party! Come on, you two, go upstairs, will you please?"

"Oh, pooh!" my mom said, sticking out her lower lip like a little kid. "We thought it would be fun to meet—"

Just then the doorbell rang.

"Jake's here!" I whispered. "Please go upstairs! Quick!"

"Come on, Tom," Mom said to Dad, taking his hand. "Let's give Claire some space."

"Thanks, Mom. Thanks, Dad," I said, totally relieved. Dad and Mom trudged across the living room and up the stairs.

I forced myself to stroll to the front door and opened it slowly. Jake stood there, grinning at me.

"Hi," he said. He wore a down vest over a heavy wool sweater, blue jeans, and sneakers. "Ready to go?" he added impatiently.

"In a minute," I said as casually as I could. "Let me get my coat."

Jake stepped in and I opened the coat closet at the bottom of the stairs. A movement at the top of the stairs caught my eye. Mom and Dad were peeking around the corner of the bannister at the top of the stairs. Mom grinned and waved.

I rolled my eyes and motioned for them to stay up there.

"Okay, Jake, let's go," I said, tugging on my coat, hoping to get out of there before my parents changed their minds and came down.

As I closed the door behind us, I looked up to see Mom and Dad sitting on the stairs halfway down, peeking through the railing. I rolled my eyes again, grinned, and stuck my tongue out at them.

Jake and I piled into the car and headed for the party.

"I'm really up for this party," Jake said.

"Yeah, me too," I said. I was still a little nervous, but so far everything was going just fine.

"I feel like just kicking back on weekends," he continued. "I work so hard during football season that when it's over, I just want to relax and go to a party or watch TV or something."

"Yeah, I see what you mean," I said.

"Football season is great, though," Jake said. "Were you there last year when I threw the winning pass in the last five seconds to win the game against North?"

"No, I didn't start going to the games until—"

"The team carried me off the field on their shoulders," Jake continued. "Man, that was a great night!"

"I bet it was!" I said. "That sounds so exciting."

"There've been some other really great games where I threw incredible passes—the coach couldn't believe them—but that one last year has to take the prize. The coach said I looked like a college player. But I like lots of sports."

"Oh, so do I!" I said. "I think my favorite is cross-country. I used to—"

"I hate cross-country!" Jake said. "It's boring—all you do is run forever. I like football, like I said, and swimming, and a little basketball. I'm good at those sports."

I didn't need to worry about my side of the conversation—Jake did all the talking for both of us! I didn't need to say a word. In fact, I wondered whether he'd continue talking if I suddenly jumped from the car. I thought maybe Jake was nervous, too, and he'd loosen up once we got to the party.

We pulled up in front of the Lawson house. There were already nearly a dozen cars lined up in front. But from the size of the house, it looked like there would be plenty of room for everyone.

We headed up the long front walk and rang

the doorbell. There was loud music playing inside the house, and for a moment, I wondered if anyone would be able to hear the bell.

But then the door was yanked open and I was staring into the face of Ben Riley. I was stunned—so stunned that I was absolutely speechless.

Ben's jaw dropped, too; he looked even more surprised than I was.

After a moment of Ben and me just standing there gawking at each other, Jake said sarcastically, "Hey, Riley. Are you going to let us in or should we hold the party on the front porch?"

"Come on in," Ben said, laughing. "Hi, Claire. I didn't know you'd be here."

"Well, I didn't know you'd be here, either. Surprise, surprise."

I was aware that Ben was watching me as I walked into the foyer. I waved to a friend of my brother's who was sitting in the living room.

"Can I take your coat?" Ben asked. "Jeff is in the kitchen fixing up some food trays, so I'm the substitute host."

"Sure, thanks," I said. I slipped off my coat and handed it to Ben.

I turned to say something to Jake, but he was gone. I finally saw him in the living room. Having thrown his coat on a chair, he was talking to his buddies.

"Oh, Ben, there you are!" Jennifer approached Ben from behind and wrapped her arms around his shoulders. She saw me and gave me a dirty look.

Jeff came in from the kitchen at that point. "There's music and dancing in the family room. Anybody want to come down? We've got food and soda down there, too."

Jake came over and tugged at my arm. "Let's go downstairs," he said. "I want to dance."

"Okay," I said, but I was a little annoyed that he *told* me he wanted to dance rather than asked me if I'd like to go. But I was still kind of dazed to be at a senior party, and a little depressed to find that Ben Riley was there with Jennifer. Still, I was determined to have fun.

Out of the corner of my eye I could see Ben watching us as Jake and I walked hand in hand across the living room. That made me feel great. If Ben could have a girlfriend, then I could have a—well, a date, too.

Jake led me to the back stairs and down into the darkened family room. Most of the lights were out and there were a lot of couples dancing to one of Madonna's faster songs. Heads were bobbing up and down all over the large room.

At the bottom of the stairs was a wet bar and stools. Several couples sat there sipping soda and hollering to be heard above the music.

"Come on," Jake said as he pulled me across the dance floor. We danced for the rest of that record and then three more songs.

Every time Jake introduced me as "The Golden Girl," I added, "My name is Claire Montgomery," but he just didn't seem to get the hint. The kids seemed impressed that I was the new Golden Girl, though, and a couple of the guys raised their eyebrows and thumped Jake on the back when he told them who I was, and that kind of made me feel good.

Then came a slow song, and Jake pulled me close to him and wrapped his arms around me.

I'd slow-danced with boys before, but never this close. You couldn't have wedged a pencil between us if you'd tried. Then he nuzzled my neck with his lips, which made me feel a little uncomfortable. I liked Jake and was flattered that he'd invited me to the party, but I didn't want him to be quite so possessive and physical. I wasn't ready for that yet. I pulled back just a little.

"What's the matter?" he asked, frowning.

"Nothing," I said. "Do you want to sit down for a while and talk? I'm kind of thirsty."

"After this dance," he said, and pulled me against him again.

Just then, Ben came up behind Jake and tapped him on the shoulder. Jake looked up, an irritated expression on his face.

"Mind if I cut in?" Ben asked.

"Oh, Ben!" I blurted out with a sense of relief. I was glad that it was so dark down there, because I could feel my face turning red. Before Jake could say anything, I said, "Sure, Ben. I'd love to dance."

Jake scowled, but left me with Ben. I wondered for a moment where Jennifer was; I didn't see her, but the room was pretty dark. She could've been anywhere. I wondered if she was watching us.

Ben pulled me to him gently and we danced close, but not plastered against each other the way Jake and I had been dancing.

"Is this your first high school party?" he asked.

"Oh, no!" I said quickly. "Are you kidding?"

"Which others have you been too?" Ben asked curiously

"Well, there was . . . uh . . . ." I stammered. Then I decided to be honest. "Well, actually, this is my second party," I said.

"Where was the first?" Ben pressed.

I winced. "Well, it was sort of at my house, I guess," I said.

"You had a party?"

"Well," I began, "Joe had a party last year—"

"And you were a guest?"

"Well, no, but I was allowed to peek in a couple of times." Ben grinned. "And wipe that smile off your face," I said, feeling a little defensive. "It's just that most of the kids in my class aren't party types."

"I see," he said, still grinning.

Actually, there'd been plenty of parties, but I hadn't been invited to them. But until now, I hadn't been the Golden Girl, either.

"Are you having fun with Jake?" Ben asked, watching my face closely.

"Oh, yes!" I said, forcing myself to sound enthusiastic.

"I didn't know you and Jake—"

"And here's my date now. Hi, Jake." I'd seen Jake approaching to cut in again. I smiled broadly, hoping that Ben would think I was delighted to get back to Jake. Ben looked a little disappointed and moved off.

"What did *he* want?" Jake asked, a note of bitterness in his voice.

"Just to say hello," I said.

"He's got his own date," Jake muttered, and wrapped himself around me again.

Fortunately, the song was over now, and I walked directly to the wet bar in the corner. Jake followed along behind.

"Get your soda and meet me in the next room," Jake said. "I want to shoot some pool. You play?"

"I haven't ever really learned," I said, "but I'd like to—"

"Well, you can watch me then," he said with a smile. "I'm real good."

"Is that so?" I asked sarcastically. "What fun."

Jake didn't seem to notice my tone of voice.

"I was the pool champ at the recreation commission tournaments two years ago," he bragged.

"That's nice," I said.

"I guess I especially like doing things I'm really good at."

"Most people do," I said.

"Like swimming," he said. "Did I ever tell you I was the fastest freestyle swimmer in ninth grade?"

Now here was a topic I could discuss. "Really? I was on the Harding Junior High swimming team—"

"Yeah," Jake interrupted. "I blew everyone else out of the water."

I glared at him and spoke in a flat voice. "Terrific," I said.

"I'll meet you in the next room," Jake said as he took off. "Hurry up, Jeff is ready to start a new pool game."

By the time I got my cola and hurried into the room, the game was already under way. Jake was intent on his playing and didn't notice me come in. In fact, he didn't notice me at all for three or four minutes, until he pulled ahead of Jeff.

Then he turned around and said, "What'd I tell you? Nobody can beat me."

Jake finished off the game quickly and turned around to the other kids. "Okay, who's willing to take me on?"

"Hey, Jake," I said, "let's go back upstairs and see what's going on."

"Naw, I want to play. Don't you want to watch?"

"Not particularly," I said softly.

He looked shocked. "What? Why not?"

"Well, I'm not interested in *watching* you play, but maybe if you'd *teach* me—"

"But you'd never be able to come close to beating me," he said. "There'd be no challenge in it for me."

"Okay," I said. "Forget it. In fact, you can forget about this whole date." And I turned around and walked out of the room.

He ran out after me. Fortunately, the hall was empty.

"What was that all about?" he asked angrily. "Why'd you say those things in front of everybody?"

I turned toward him abruptly. "I thought you were a nice guy, Jake. All the girls want to go out with you, and I was really happy that you'd invited me to this party. But ever since you picked me up tonight, you've done nothing but talk constantly about yourself. *Constantly!* You brag about your athletic tal-

126

ents, you insist on doing what *you* want to do, and you show absolutely no interest in anybody else! The only reason you asked me out was because I'm the Golden Girl—"

"That's not true," he protested.

"Then explain to me why you've introduced me to everyone tonight as 'The Golden Girl' and not as Claire Montgomery."

He glared at me. "This Golden Girl job has really gone to your head, hasn't it?" he said. "You think you're pretty important all of a sudden. Well, maybe you're right. I probably wouldn't have asked you out if you weren't the Golden Girl. I wanted to see what kind of a person you are underneath that new hairdo, and I've found out—"

"How could you have found out anything about me?" I cried. "You haven't asked me one question about myself for the past hour and a half!"

"You're a spoiled, self-centered girl who needs to be the center of attention—"

"I am?" I gasped, unable to believe my ears.

"You were nothing before you got the Golden Girl job," he said, "Nobody knew you were alive."

I stared at him, clenching my fists so that I wouldn't say anything more, my face hot with anger.

"Will you at least take me home?" I asked him finally.

Jake stalked upstairs, grabbed our coats, shoved mine at me, and headed out to the car.

We didn't speak all the way home. "Don't bother seeing me to the door," I said when we pulled up in front of my house.

"I wouldn't think of it," he snarled.

I slammed the car door and he roared off into the night. I watched the car's taillights grow smaller and fainter, until they disappeared completely.

I trudged up the porch steps and into the house. My parents, who were reading in the living room, looked up, surprised, when I walked in.

"My goodness, that was a short party," my mom said, glancing at her watch. "Was it fun?"

"A riot," I said, and flopped down on the nearest chair.

"Feel like talking about it?" Mom asked.

"I think I'll join a convent when I grow up," I said.

"Oh, honey, you don't want to do that," Mom said with a small smile.

"Boys!" I said. "Who needs them? I hate them. I'll never go out on a date again. I'll grow up and become a famous doctor and discover a cure for cancer and never think about boys again."

"That would be nice, honey," Mom said. "I

mean, the part about finding a cure for cancer. Or maybe for now you could volunteer as a candy striper at the hospital—"

"Maybe not, Mom," I said. "I just want to get boys out of my life. I've sworn off them forever."

"If that's what you want . . ." Mom said.

"That's what I want," I said. "They're all so immature. Every one of them . . . except you, Dad."

"Well, that's a relief," he said calmly, puffing on his pipe.

I walked upstairs and fell into bed.

That's it, I told myself. *I'll do the best job I can being Trent's Golden Girl. I'll concentrate on a brilliant career in medicine—and no more boys!*

Chapter Ten

"Wow, I hear you really lost it at the party," Audrey said when I saw her on Monday morning. As usual, she was waiting at my locker for the weekend update.

"What did you hear?" I asked her, not sure I wanted to hear what she had to say.

"Well, for one thing, I heard that you were bragging about your Golden Girl job on Friday night."

"What!" I exclaimed.

"Yeah, and they said that you were mad at Jake for not paying more attention to you, and that you and Jake had an incredible argument. I can't believe you took your soda and poured it over Jake's head while you screamed awful names at him."

"You've got to be kidding!" I gasped, astounded by the vile rumors that were circulating about me.

Audrey solemnly shook her head.

"Oh, that's terrific," I cried. "Just what I need!" I sighed. "You know something? I would never have thought that I'd say this, but I'm not sure this Golden Girl job is worth it. I've never been so miserable! No one ever spread vicious rumors about me before.."

"You mean, the story isn't true?" Audrey was surprised .

"Of course not!" I said.

"Well, I didn't think it sounded like the Claire Montgomery I know," she said. "But then, people do change—"

"If my best friend believed it, I guess everyone else will, too," I said pointedly.

"I'm sorry," Audrey said. "I should've known better."

"Well, yes, you should have," I said irritably. "Or at least, you should have called and asked me about it. Why is this *happening* to me!" I cried out in desperation.

"Public figures always get dumped on. Just ask any celebrity," Audrey said.

"Next time I meet a celebrity, I'll do just that," I said.

The *Lincoln High School Sentinel* was passed out at the end of classes on Monday afternoon. It's usually a good paper, and most of the kids read it cover to cover. One of the most popular columns, "Tasty Tidbits," usually hints, without using names, about who is dating who in school.

I picked up my copy and ducked into the library to browse through it before heading home. I sat at one of the wooden tables behind the card catalog.

I read the first page and opened the paper to "Tasty Tidbits," hoping to escape for a few minutes in the school gossip. The opening paragraph caught my eye. "We hear that a certain sophomore girl who's recently made it big has turned into a snob," it read. "Lincoln High School's new TV personality is said to think a lot of herself these days and is turning off friends right and left."

I gasped and threw the paper down on the table in front of me. "Why are they *doing* this to me?" I said out loud. "What have I done to make people so mad at me?"

I picked up the paper again and reread the part about me. It had to be about me—I was the only sophomore "TV personality" at school.

I got up then and paced around the library, muttering to myself.

This Golden Girl job isn't glamorous, I thought, *not at all.* Then I remembered what Audrey had said. I stopped pacing. Maybe, I thought, it wasn't just me. Maybe every girl who'd been the Golden Girl had been talked and gossiped about. I was just a good target.

I was beginning to feel slightly more in

control. I picked up my coat and books and headed down the hallway. As luck would have it, Ben Riley was walking in my direction. I ducked back into the library to avoid him, but after a moment he appeared in the doorway.

"Hi, Claire," he said.

"Hi."

"Would you mind if I stopped by your house tonight?"

"Would I mind—uh, no, not at all," I said. "What's up?"

"I'd like to talk with you, maybe go for a walk," Ben said. "At about seven?"

"I'll be ready," I said. "See you then."

Ben turned and disappeared down the hall.

What could Ben possibly want? Wasn't I doing a good job? Mr. Trent seemed to be pleased when we shot the commercial. Maybe he had changed his mind about me. I couldn't imagine any other reason why Ben would want to come and see me.

My stomach growled just as the doorbell rang. I'd been so concerned about Ben wanting to see me that I'd told Mom I didn't want supper. My stomach was hungry, but the rest of me wasn't in the mood for food.

I opened the door and there stood Ben. He was wearing a black leather jacket and jeans. As he smiled, his eyes sparkled, and I realized that I'd almost forgotten how good-looking he was. How could I have forgotten?

And I was going to give up boys!

"Hi," he said. "Ready to go?"

"Ready," I said as I grabbed my coat from the closet. He opened the door as I put on my coat.

"Better wear a scarf or hat," he said. "It's pretty cold outside tonight."

I pulled my woolen hat off the closet shelf and put it on, and we walked out onto the front porch.

"I'm glad you could come," Ben said as we descended the front steps.

"Is there anything wrong?" I asked.

"No, why?" Ben said, his dark eyebrows knitted together, frowning.

"Oh, I mean, I thought maybe you wanted to talk to me about the Golden Girl job."

Ben stopped and gazed at me. "I asked you to go for a walk because . . . well, because I wanted to tell you how angry I was about the 'Tidbits' column in the paper today. It was so petty and unfair."

I smiled, relieved—and touched. "Thanks, Ben. I needed that. And I appreciate your support."

He looked surprised. "You seem to be handling it well."

I laughed. "You should've seen me three

hours ago! I wasn't exactly mellow about it then."

"It's just jealousy," he said, moving closer to me as we walked along. I could feel his arm swinging gently next to mine, his shoulder level with my ear.

"I keep telling myself that," I said. "My head understands, but my heart isn't listening. I guess it still hurts a little."

"Let's walk in the park," he said. We were passing the City Park entrance, and he veered to the left and I followed.

Ben was right. It was quite cold out, and tiny flakes of snow were beginning to fall from the violet sky. The moon was just barely visible behind the shadow of a cloud. I shivered.

"Cold?" he asked.

"Just a little," I said. "But it's a pretty night."

Then Ben took my hand and squeezed it gently. "Yes, it is a pretty night." After a moment, he asked, "You aren't going with Jake Duncan, are you?"

I couldn't help but laugh. "Are you kidding?"

Ben glanced at me, surprised. "No, why?"

I stopped and turned to him, still holding his hand. "You didn't hear about our argument at the party?"

Ben gazed up into the sky a moment before he answered. "Well," he said thoughtfully, "I heard something about your wanting more attention for being the Golden Girl, but I figured that was just gossip."

I was amazed. "You did? How did you know it wasn't true?"

Ben grinned, then he touched the tip of my nose with his finger. "Because I *know* you, Claire. A lot of other girls would've let the Golden Girl job go to their heads, but you would never do something like that."

I smiled up at him. "Thanks, Ben."

"For what?"

"For not believing those rumors—and for believing in me."

"So you're definitely not going out with Jake?"

"Not unless it's out to a boxing ring to punch each other out."

Ben laughed and leaned closer. "I'm glad," he said softly.

He gently kissed me then, his lips warm and soft. Then he kissed me again.

I pulled back a little. "But what about Jennifer?" I asked.

"What do you mean?" he said.

"Well, she was at the party with you," I said. "And at the basketball game she told me that I was supposed to stay away from you."

Ben looked disgusted. "She did? I thought something was up when I saw her talking to you."

"Well?" I asked. "Is she or isn't she?"

"Is she or isn't she what?" he asked.

I gave him a playful shove. "Your girlfriend, dummy."

He shoved me back, grinning. "What's it to you, Montgomery?"

I pushed him back, and we startled wrestling there in the park with the snow coming down all around us, our shrieks of laughter echoing through the nearby woods. The moon seemed to smile faintly through the limbs of a huge oak tree.

My foot caught on an exposed tree root and I fell to the ground, and Ben collapsed on top of me.

"Okay, I give up!" I shouted.

Ben offered me a hand, and pulled me up from the ground.

"I think you could punch Jake out if you really wanted to," Ben said, grinning.

"Oh, and you haven't even seen my mean left hook," I said, laughing. "But you still haven't answered my question."

"Which was—"

"Oh, you're going to make me repeat it, eh?" I looked up at him seriously. "What about Jennifer? Is she your girlfriend?"

Ben gazed at me. "Right now, I don't want to talk about Jennifer, okay?"

"But, I thought that you and she—"

"Let's not spoil the night," Ben insisted. "I'll talk to you about her later."

As Ben took my hand, I felt a blush warm my face. I couldn't seem to stop smiling.

Ben put his arms around me. "Not tonight," he repeated softly. I stood up on my toes and kissed him. He kissed me back then, long and hard, before I pushed him gently away.

"Why did you stop?" he whispered. "What's wrong?"

"Nothing," I said, and gazed up at him. "But I don't want to get too involved until you're ready to tell me more about your relationship with Jennifer."

"Let's start back now. We'll talk soon," he promised, as he took my hand and led me back home.

Chapter Eleven

I tried not to think about commentating Trent's upcoming fashion show. Every time it crossed my mind, I got a jittery stomach, sweaty palms, and a pounding heart.

But soon I couldn't ignore it anymore. The show was scheduled for a Friday night, and Ben had given me the commentator's cards and told me to practice in front of a mirror at home.

"Just relax, pretend you're performing for the TV camera, and have fun," he said when he handed me the cards.

"Right," I said. "And then I'll step out on the stage in front of hundreds of people and I'll faint."

"You'll have a rehearsal the day before the show," Ben said. "Just practice the way you do for the commercials, and you'll be ready. I have faith in you."

"I wish I did," I said.

It had been a week since Ben and I had taken the walk in the park. We'd seen each other in the halls at school and at a videotaping of another commercial. Ben was friendly and funny when we were together, but he hadn't kissed me or mentioned Jennifer since that snowy night in the park. And I hadn't pushed him for an explanation. I figured that if he wanted our relationship to grow, he would explain when he was ready.

That isn't to say that I didn't daydream about Ben, or that I wasn't dying to find out what was going on with him and Jennifer. But I didn't bother him with it, and I felt a kind of comfortable satisfaction with simply working near Ben.

I tried Ben's suggestion of practicing in front of a mirror. That helped a little, I think, but the thought of repeating it in front of a mob of people made me tremble all over.

I even made my family sit in the living room and listen to me read from the cards.

"And here is Susie wearing the latest in Trent's spring fashions. Her coral silk blouse is trimmed with pearl buttons—"

And Joe would whistle like an idiot from the "audience" on the couch and shout out, "All right, Susie! What a babe!"

Need I say more? It was impossible.

The day before the show there was a rehearsal in a banquet room in the mall basement. There was no runway there, but we practiced on the floor. As I read the cards from the podium, the models walked through their paces as if they were onstage, showing off their clothes for the audience.

"Smile, girls! Smile!" called the fashion show coordinator, Mrs. Casum, as the girls floated across the stage.

During one of her jaunts across the floor, one of the junior high girls tripped and lunged forward a few feet, a horrified expression on her face.

"Girls, if one of you trips like Terri did just now, keep going, keep going!" Mrs. Casum said. We were standing around in small groups, listening to her read notes she'd taken during the run-through. "Even if you fall on the stage, just smile, get up, and keep on going!"

"Don't plant the suggestion in my mind," I muttered. "I will not trip, I will not trip," I repeated to myself.

"You won't, you won't," a voice said from behind me.

I turned around to see Ben grinning at me.

"Ben! I'm so glad you came," I said. "I really need your moral support."

"You don't need anything," he reassured me, rubbing my shoulders gently. "Just relax."

"Relax, girls," Mrs. Casum said. "And have fun."

"That's good advice," Ben whispered in my ear. "You're going to be great."

"I wish I had your confidence," I said, shaking my head. My body began to tremble again.

In twenty-four hours, it would be all over. And I'd either be a "professional" for doing a good job—or a laughingstock for messing up the entire show.

Just twenty-four hours to go—I didn't know if I was going to make it.

The fashion show was scheduled for seven on Friday evening. I managed to make it through the day at school, but my stomach was filled with butterflies. I don't think I heard anything my teachers said all day, but I pretended to look alert in math.

I couldn't eat supper that night. I told Mom that I'd eat after the show if I survived it. She just hugged me and told me that she and Dad would be there and that they'd be rooting for me.

I arrived at the mall at six, dressed in a khaki linen suit and a pale peach blouse, compliments of Trent's Department Store. I wore my hair pulled up on top of my head, with soft tendrils falling loose around my ears. I'd tucked a tissue into my pocket to wipe my sweaty palms, and now I whipped it out and blotted my hands so I could shake Mr. Trent's hand when I saw him.

I was so jittery, I wobbled a little on my

high heels as I rounded the corner and the runway came into view. It had been assembled that afternoon in the middle of the mall courtyard for the show, and the people who'd set it up were just leaving.

Mr. Trent, in a dark blue suit, was standing with Ben next to the runway platform. He turned to me and smiled nervously when he saw me.

"Well, young lady," Mr. Trent said, "I'm certainly counting on you to be a smash success tonight. I hope you aren't as nervous as I am."

"I'm at least as nervous as you are, Mr. Trent," I said, ignoring Ben's wink. "But I'll do my best."

Mr. Trent's face turned white. "You're nervous? You don't look nervous. Are you sure you're up to this?"

"You bet," I lied.

"Well, I hope so," Mr. Trent fretted. "I guess I'll go check on some details with Mrs. Casum. If you'll excuse me?"

"Of course," I said. Ben and I watched him stride off toward the store.

Ben grinned. "Dad said he's always like this before a fashion show. But after the show, he'll come around and tell you that you're the best Golden Girl he's ever had."

I sighed. "I hope he has reason to say that."

"Of course he will," Ben said, putting a hand on my shoulder. "Just relax."

"Sure, sure," I said. "Uh, Ben, if you don't mind, I think I'd like to be by myself for a little while, just to try and calm myself down."

"Sure," he said. He gently kissed my cheek and disappeared around the side of the platform.

I went to the ladies' room, combed my hair, and fixed my makeup. I made sure my hose were pulled up tight so they wouldn't bag, and checked my watch for a third time. It was now 6:20.

I walked out of the ladies' room and strolled over to the runway platform.

Ben walked up behind me. "Go up on the platform," he said, "and stand behind the podium to get the feel of it."

"Good idea," I said, and started up the steps to the platform.

Halfway up the stairs I banged my knee hard on the step in front of me.

"Ouch! Oh, great! Wonderful start, just wonderful!" I cried out.

"Hey, Claire," Ben said, "you're okay, you just tripped. That won't happen during the show."

"How do *you* know?" I demanded angrily. "I told you I didn't want to do this! I told you I wouldn't be any good and that I'd be nervous! I'll probably ruin the whole thing!"

Ben stood there at the bottom of the stairs and stared at me, obviously surprised by my outburst.

"Claire," he said calmly, "I think I'd better leave you alone now. I'll see you after the show. Good luck." He turned and walked away.

I knew Ben was just trying to help. I opened my mouth to stop him, then realized that he was probably right: I was nervous and upset and not in the mood for anything other than getting through this show. I'd apologize to him later on.

I walked up to the top of the runway and over to the podium. I stood there and looked out over the two hundred or so seats that had been set up below. There were people arriving already to get good seats. I watched them, and I had to admit that they didn't look too scary.

I walked carefully down the steps from the platform and back to the models' dressing room. Most of the models were already wearing their first outfit. A sign in each dressing area read DON'T GET WRINKLED! DO NOT SIT DOWN WHILE WEARING CLOTHES! The models were standing around chatting with each other, and they didn't seem at all nervous.

I checked my watch. It was a quarter to seven. Mr. Trent walked by and gave me the thumbs-up sign, and I suddenly felt nauseated.

"I can't do this," I muttered to myself. I

paced back and forth for a few minutes, then walked back to the ladies' room again. The nausea had vanished, but my breathing was irregular and my heart was pounding.

I stood in front of the mirror and fussed with my hair.

"Just relax," I said to my reflection. "Just—" *Hic!* My mouth dropped open. "Oh, no!" I cried out. The—*hic!*—hiccups! "I've got to find Ben," I said, and ran out of the ladies' room.

Hic! Hic! Hic!

"Where's Ben Riley?" I asked one of the models near the dressing area.

"Ben who?" she asked.

Hic!

I ran on past the edge of the platform, but I heard the model gasp, "She's got the hiccups!" The mall courtyard was nearly filled with people, all anxious for the show to begin.

Hic! Hic! Hic!

"Where's Ben Riley?" I asked Mrs. Casum, who was walking hurriedly toward the platform with a clipboard in her hand.

"I think I saw him in the dressing area," she said. "But it's time to start. Are you ready?"

Hic! "I have to talk to Ben." *Hic!*

Mrs. Casum's eyes widened when she heard the hiccups. "Are you going to be all right?" she asked.

"I have to talk to Ben," I repeated. *Hic!*

146

"There he is," Mrs. Casum said, pointing to a corner of the dressing area.

Models turned to watch as I ran by. "She has the hiccups!" I heard several of them whisper to each other.

"Ben, Ben, I can't do it! *Hic*!" I said. "I have the hiccups! You'll have to call off the show or get someone else to—"

Ben grabbed me by the shoulders, and kissed me long and hard on my mouth. I was so shocked, and so pleased at this sudden show of affection, that I relaxed immediately and let myself melt against him. I put my arms around him and felt his strong back muscles. His lips were soft and warm.

"You look beautiful," he said, gently pulling away. "I've been meaning to tell you."

"Thanks, Ben," I said.

"Hiccups gone?" he asked, smiling.

I suddenly realized that I hadn't hiccuped at all since we'd kissed.

"They *are* gone!" I exclaimed happily.

Ben grinned. "See, I *told* you I had a sure-fire way to stop the hiccups. Now go up there and do your job. Everyone's waiting."

I turned around and saw that Mrs. Casum, Mr. Trent, and Mr. Riley were standing at the dressing room door, watching us. "Her hiccups are gone!" they said and began to applaud.

I laughed and blushed and laughed some

more. I think I'll remember that moment more clearly than any from the fashion show itself.

I climbed the stairs to the platform, receiving dozens of "good luck" thumps on my back as I passed.

I walked to the podium, switched on the microphone, and said in a clear, strong voice, "Good evening, ladies and gentlemen. Welcome to Trent's fourteenth annual spring fashion show. I'm so glad you all could come."

It was over before I knew it. The audience loved it, and I not only survived but I did a good job—and my hiccups were history.

Mr. Trent and Mr. Riley came over and pumped my hand and told me what a great job I'd done.

"You're the best Golden Girl we've ever had," Mr. Trent said, beaming. "Splendid job, splendid!"

Ben stood off to the side and mouthed the word, "See?" When his father and Mr. Trent left, he came over and wrapped his arms around me.

"You were great, Claire," he said. "You were professional and poised, just the way you are on camera."

"Once you helped me stop my hiccups," I said, laughing. "By the way, Ben, I liked your method. Great technique."

Ben smiled down at me. Then he kissed me gently.

I heard a little cry behind me and turned to see Jennifer standing there. She glared at Ben. "So this is why you broke up with me. I should've known." She turned in a huff and stalked off.

"Is she okay?" I asked.

Ben smiled. "She's used to getting what she wants," he said. "She'll be all right. I never really considered her to be my girlfriend. We went out a few times and she started acting as if she owned me. I've been trying to explain my feelings to her for months. I tried to tell her the night of Jeff's party, but she just wouldn't listen. I think she didn't realize it was over until this very moment."

"Is that why you seemed bothered when Betty at the cosmetics counter asked about her? Because you were trying to break up with her?" I asked.

Ben nodded. "Partly," he said. "But I've been trying to impress my father. I want him to think I can be professional about this job. I thought if people started talking about me going out with the Golden Girl, he'd think I wasn't attending to business. It was hard staying away from you." He grinned. "But I guess I didn't try very hard."

I laughed. "Well, how do you think your

father felt when he saw you kiss me before the show?"

"He thought it was great. He really likes you. See what I mean?" He nodded toward his father, who was standing at the edge of the crowd. Mr. Riley grinned and waved. "I think he knows I can handle the job and still be involved with the Golden Girl."

I gathered up my coat and Ben walked with me out to the parking lot, where I was supposed to meet my parents.

"It's a beautiful night," Ben said. "Spring is in the air—you can smell it." He took my hand. "Your performances just keep getting better and better," he said. "You're going to have a career on television one day, I think."

"I had a pretty good coach," I said, smiling. "Besides, I'd planned on becoming a doctor."

"Whatever you decide to do, you'll do well. Why, if you become a doctor, then you'll have a really suave bedside manner," Ben said. He kissed me gently and whispered, "And I hope I'll be there to tell you how proud I am of you."

Sweet Dreams

We hope you enjoyed reading this book. If you would like to receive further information about available titles in the Bantam series, just write to the address below, with your name and address: Kim Prior, Bantam Books, 61–63 Uxbridge Road, Ealing, London W5 5SA.

If you live in Australia or New Zealand and would like more information about the series, please write to:

Sally Porter
Transworld Publishers
(Australia) Pty Ltd
15–23 Helles Avenue
Moorebank
NSW 2170
AUSTRALIA

Kiri Martin
Transworld Publishers (NZ) Ltd
Cnr. Moselle and Waipareira
Avenues
Henderson
Auckland
NEW ZEALAND

All Bantam and Young Adult books are available at your bookshop or newsagent, or can be ordered at the following address: Corgi/Bantam Books, Cash Sales Department, PO Box 11, Falmouth, Cornwall, TR10 9EN.

Please list the title(s) you would like, and send together with a cheque or postal order. You should allow for the cost of book(s) plus postage and packing charges as follows:
80p for one book
£1.00 for two books
£1.20 for three books
£1.40 for four books
Five or more books free.

Please note that payment must be made in pounds sterling; other currencies are unacceptable.

(The above applies to readers in the UK and Republic of Ireland only)

BFPO customers, please allow for the cost of the book(s) plus the following for postage and packing: 80p for the first book, and 20p for each additional copy.

Overseas customers, please allow £1.50 for postage and packing for the first book, £1.00 for the second book, and 30p for each subsequent title ordered.

SWEET VALLEY HIGH

The top-selling teenage series starring identical twins Jessica and Elizabeth Wakefield and all their friends at Sweet Valley High. One new title every month!

SWEET VALLEY SUPER STARS

PEN PALS

by Sharon Dennis Wyeth

How do four boy-crazy girls meet four girl-crazy boys?
They place an ad for PEN PALS, of course! Well, that's
what Lisa, Shanon, Amy and Palmer (otherwise known
as the Foxes) do – and it's not long before they get a reply!
An irresistibly entertaining new series.

1. BOYS WANTED
2. TOO CUTE FOR WORDS
3. P.S. FORGET IT!
4. NO CREEPS NEED APPLY
5. SAM THE SHAM

Forthcoming titles:

6. AMY'S SONG
7. HANDLE WITH CARE
8. SEALED WITH A KISS

THE SEBASTIAN SISTERS

Susan Beth Pfeffer

An compelling series that follows the fortunes of four sisters – Evvie, Thea, Claire and Sybil – as each reaches the landmark of a sixteenth birthday and must face up to new challenges and relationships.

'Fairly sparkles with romance . . . the Sebastians have established themselves as a family to watch' PUBLISHERS WEEKLY

Available now:

1. EVVIE AT SIXTEEN

Forthcoming titles:

2. THEA AT SIXTEEN
3. CLAIRE AT SIXTEEN
4. SYBIL AT SIXTEEN
5. MEG AT SIXTEEN